Bob Moats

I0567953

Doyle's Paradise

Rev. 1001140950p

1

Doyle's Paradise

For information and address:
Magic 1 Productions
P.O. Box 524, Fraser MI 48026-0524
Website: http://murdernovels.com
Cover by Bob Moats

Extra special thanks to:

Special thanks to Susan Haughton who edited this book and for her great suggestions.

Thanks to the beta readers Cindy Gross Valstad, Al Norris, Bill Sandy, Rebecca Hester, Janet Lawson, Sherry Tull, Fleur Wilkinson, Deborah Gauze, and Amy Morningstar

Thank you to all the people who purchased this book. I hope you enjoy it as much as I enjoyed writing it for my faithful readers.

The Jim Richards Family of Readers is listed in the back of the book.

Doyle's Paradise by Bob Moats

Chapter 1

Doyle stood looking out the front window of his office on Michigan Avenue in Detroit. He was watching the slow moving traffic on the road, as he thought about his vacation to Hawaii with his lady friend, Poppy. They had asked Marge, his secretary, to go along with them. So, it would be an interesting trip.

His partner in the private investigations firm was Oscar Drew. Oscar had said he wanted to go visit relatives in New York. So it would be just Doyle, Poppy, and Marge winging their way to paradise. Doyle decided to use the recovery fee they got for finding the stolen Egyptian artifacts on their last case for the art gallery, and take a much needed vacation. In all of his years on the Detroit police force as a detective, he never took time off.

"Are you daydreaming, Arthur?" Marge asked from her desk by the front door.

"I'm naked on the beaches of paradise, the sun beating down on me, and the wind billowing my hair," he replied.

"Well, if I'm going along, I would appreciate you not getting naked. And you don't have enough hair to billow," she retorted.

"I can dream, right?" he said with a smile, and turned to her desk. "Have you made the arrangements?"

"I got the airline tickets booked. As for Hawaii, I don't know where we are going yet, not until we get there," she replied.

"I found an online website for a nice little island off the smaller island of Oahu, just a jump from the main island of Hawaii. It's secluded, no phone towers, internet, or television to distract us. One week of solitude and peace. Cut off from civilization. No worries, no stress, no crime. It will be so nice."

"I hope they at least have a radio station. I may go crazy if I can't hear something."

"Are you taking your knitting?"

"Of course. I can rest on the beach and knit a bikini for Poppy," she said, with a grin.

Doyle laughed. "I'm sure she'll enjoy that. You do know you'll have to put your knitting needles in your luggage. They won't let you on the plane with them in your carry-on bags."

Doyle's Paradise

"I already checked on that, so I'll pack them away. I don't want to be accused of hijacking the plane with a number three knitting needle."

Again, Doyle laughed. He looked to the back door as it opened, and in came Oscar, the firm's second investigator.

"Hey, Oscar, what's up?"

"My blood pressure," he said with a frown. "I called my brother in New York and he wasn't very friendly. I know I haven't talked to him in a number of years, but he didn't have to be rude."

"If it's that bad, you can go with us to Hawaii," Doyle offered.

"No, I have lots of relatives out there to go visit. I can just ignore him," Oscar said. 'When are you scheduled to go?"

Doyle looked at Marge. She said, "Got us booked for the day after tomorrow. I called Poppy and told her. This will give us a day to get packed and ready."

"Thanks, Marge," he smiled. "So Oscar, are you flying to New York or driving?"

"Driving, of course. It's not that far and I can leave from there at a moment's notice. My family is a little odd. So, it's an excuse to see my mother, the only sane one in the bunch. The rest of the relatives, I can do without."

"Sounds like you'll have a splendid time," Doyle said, sarcastically.

"No, I won't, but at least no one can say I didn't visit." Oscar went to his desk and picked up the envelope sitting on it. He opened it and smiled. "Thank you, Art. I appreciate this," he said as he pulled out the check.

"It's extra pay for your help with the stolen statues," Doyle explained. "Don't spend it all in one place."

"I'll blow it on beer and women in New York City. I haven't been there since I was a young man running the streets. I still remember a few places where I can get into trouble."

"Just don't try and call me to bail you out. I'll be in seclusion. Cut off from all communications and civilization on a private island in the Pacific. What a glorious week it will be."

"Sounds crazy," Oscar said. "You'll be climbing the walls by day three."

The front door opened and in walked Poppy Drake, Doyle's latest girlfriend. He had gone through three women in the last month, so he hoped she would stay around longer than a month. He wasn't having much luck with women. Not that he worried about it, he enjoyed the romps in bed with them. He would still like a relationship with a good woman. Poppy seemed to fit in nicely.

"Hey beautiful, how are you?" he asked as she came over to him and put her arms around him.

She kissed his lips and said, "Better now. You have that effect on me." She backed up and said hello to Marge. She looked back to Oscar at his desk and said, "Oscar, are you sure you don't want to go with us?"

"I may change my mind, but so far I'm going in the other direction. The East Coast is my destination."

"I'll leave the information for where we'll be if you do decide to come out. You can't call me there to ask where we'll be." Doyle said.

"Where will we be, by the way?" Poppy asked.

Doyle told her about the island. She smiled through his description. "So, if we are cut off from the rest of the world, how do we leave if we are not happy with the accommodations?"

"Swim, I guess," Doyle said, with a sly smile.

"Swim with the sharks? No, thank you," Poppy grimaced. "I hope they have a boat."

"The information I got was they were totally cut off. Just one plane to drop off and pick up guests, and there's just one ship to deliver fuel for the generators, and food for everyone. But the boat only sails in once a month with supplies."

"I guess we'll be really alone in paradise," Poppy said. "What about medical emergencies?"

"They have an on-site doctor and a small clinic for people who get poison ivy or worse. They have it all covered. This is a place to get away from it all."

"Get away from civilization, yes. It sounds good, but also sounds ominous. No connection to the outside world, that sounds dangerous," Poppy said.

"Only if you let it be dangerous. However, I'm taking my gun with me, in my luggage, just in case. So, I'm not worrying too much."

"The Island of Dr. Moreau," Marge said, from her desk.

"What?" Doyle asked.

"A book by H.G. Wells, about a crazy scientist who experimented on humans, crossing them with animals. They were on a secluded island, too," she replied.

"I saw that movie," Poppy said. She turned back to Doyle. "This better not be an island of crazy experiments performed on us."

"I highly doubt it. Besides, I'm the only one who can perform crazy experiments on you. They have a website and nothing was said about human experiments."

"You really think they would advertise that they'd turn us into goats or pigs?"

"I'm sure they wouldn't. Now, let's get our heads back on our vacation trip to paradise, and forget all that horror stuff. I'm going to enjoy this trip even if I have to turn into a goat or pig." Doyle went to his desk and sat.

"You'd make a lousy goat, but I can see you as a pig," Poppy said.

Doyle gave her the finger and smiled.

*

Chapter 2

Doyle asked Oscar to make up a nice sign to put on the door explaining that they would be out of town for a week. Oscar put the sign up and then went over to Doyle. Poppy was sitting with Marge going over the website on her computer for the island they would be staying at.

"I'm going to head out," Oscar said. "I want to get a jump on going East. I'm not fond of those freeways and toll roads. I called my mom and told her I was coming out, she's pleased. At least she is. I'm not looking forward to visiting some of my relatives, but I know mom will have a big to-do get-together when I get there."

"You have a father?" Doyle asked.

"He was a cop in Brooklyn, shot and killed during a robbery. That's why my mother wasn't happy when I became a cop, too. But I'd call her once a month to let her know I was still alive. If I missed a call, she would call me. My mother worries too much."

"Sorry about your father. You did tell her you were a P.I. now?"

Doyle's Paradise

"Oh sure, she likes that better than me being a cop. I told her all I do is follow cheating spouses. She even warned me to avoid getting shot by some husband cheating on his wife."

"I don't think that will happen too often," Doyle said with a grin.

Doyle and Oscar looked over at the two women laughing at the computer. Marge raised her head and said, "Arthur, you're in luck. They do have an area where you can swim and sunbathe in the nude. Now if you can let your hair billow, it will complete your daydream."

Doyle just smiled, and remained silent. Poppy gave him a wink and the women went back to the computer.

"Sure, Oscar, take off. It's still early, so you can beat the worst of the traffic."

"Thanks, I'll see you in a week. Don't sunburn anything personal," he said with a grin and gave his goodbyes to Marge and Poppy. He went out the back door as Doyle stood and went to the women.

"So, what do you think, besides the nude beaches?" he asked them.

"It looks fine to me," Poppy said. "I didn't see any half human, half goat people running around in the photos."

"They don't advertise that in the brochure," Marge said, with a grin.

"You two are a riot. Let's close up and go home to pack," he said and turned back to his desk.

"Are you taking your Indiana Jones hat?" Marge asked.

He looked at the hat hanging on the wall. "Yeah, it'll fit in with where we're going. I'll take it." He reached out and took the hat down and placed it on his head. Poppy laughed. "What's so funny?" he asked her.

"I was just picturing you nude, wearing your hat," she said with a sly grin.

"That's it, I'm leaving. Anyone still here when I go, can stay here." He started heading for the back door as he heard chairs scrape the floor and quick footfalls. The two women rushed past him and out the door. "That's better," he said.

Marge got to her car and said, "See you Friday morning. Are we meeting here or at the airport?"

Doyle's Paradise

"Here will be good, we can ride together in a cab so we don't have to fight traffic to Metro airport."

"Good, see you then. Eight sharp, our plane departs at ten. You know how long it takes to get out to the airport on the freeway," she said and got into her car.

"Are you going home to pack?" Doyle asked Poppy.

"I'm already packed. Everything is in the car. I plan on staying with you until we leave."

"Wow, I feel honored. A houseguest. Shall we go pack my stuff?"

"I intend to pack your stuff," She said with a sly grin and got in her car. Doyle followed her out of the parking lot and over to his apartment.

"I'll leave my bags in the car and we can move them when we go."

"Works for me," he said as they went to his apartment.

"You do have luggage? I mean you haven't taken a vacation in a lot of years, but you must have something?"

"I thought of just throwing everything in garbage bags. That way the luggage handlers can throw them around and not break anything. I used to have yellow toxic waste bags, but they're gone now."

"You saw that on TV didn't you?"

"Yep, Rizzoli and Isles." He went to his bedroom and opened a closet. He took out two Samsonite suitcases, brand new and unused. "I bought these last week when we talked about going away. I never had luggage, so I figured it was time."

Poppy went to his clothes closet and started pulling out shirts. "Do you only have white button down shirts?"

"Those are my work shirts," he said and opened the other side of the closet. "These are my fun in the sun clothes."

She pulled out a couple wild print shirts. "Do you actually wear these?"

"Only once, during a wild Tahitian party at a local bar. I was a hit. The flower shirt got me a lot of comments."

"And a lot of snickers behind your back."

Doyle's Paradise

"Hey, these will look great in Hawaii. As a matter of fact, leave that one out. I'll wear it on the plane."

"I'm not sitting next to you."

"Fine, sit next to a screaming baby."

"Better than sitting next to your screaming shirt." Poppy put the shirt on the bed and went through the rest of his clothes. "You don't have any shorts?"

"You've seen my legs, I don't want to offend anyone."

"True, apes have less hair." She gave him a smile and said, "Hey, why don't we take a bath together and I'll shave your legs."

Doyle paused, mulling over the thought. "We'll see. Now let's finish packing."

They spent the next hour packing his suitcases and Doyle put them by the front door. "Now, what do we do for the next thirty-one hours?"

"Use your imagination," she said and pulled him back to the bedroom.

Friday morning came early after the whole day they spent in bed since they finished packing his things. Doyle was energized and Poppy was dragging.

"I think I got lazy doing nothing," she said.

"Well, in a couple hours we will be boarding the plane to paradise. Now go take a shower and wake up."

"Want to take one with me?"

"I already took one. I woke about an hour ago and got my day organized. I took your keys and put your luggage with mine in the car to go to the office to meet Marge. Then we'll call for the cab ride from there."

"Okay, if I'm not out in an hour come rescue me. I'll be asleep in the tub."

Doyle laughed as she went to the bathroom. He finished getting his apartment ready to be vacant for a week, and then Poppy came out looking all fresh and renewed.

"Well, you bounce back quite well," he said as she came over to him and gave him a kiss. "Are you ready to go now? We have to meet Marge in twenty minutes."

"I'm ready if you are," she replied.

They went out to Doyle's car and drove to the office one more time. He parked in the back next to Marge's car.

"I hope you don't mind, I already called a cab. They can be so slow at times," Marge said.

"It's good with me, you're more organized about these things than I am," Doyle said.

"I just like taking care of the details," she replied.

A few minutes later, a cab pulled into the parking lot and over to them. They packed the luggage in the cab trunk and got in.

"Metro Airport, please," Doyle said and the cab pulled out.

*

Chapter 3

"What terminal?" the cab driver asked.

Doyle looked at Marge, "Well?"

"Oh, American Airlines, please," she told the driver. He headed over to the I-94 freeway.

"How long is the flight?" Poppy asked Doyle.

Doyle looked at Marge again, "Well?"

Marge grinned, "You don't know much, do you, Arthur?"

He laughed, "I'm not a fountain of information like you are, Marge. Besides you arranged the flight. How long is the flight?"

"About five hours to LA, then transfer to a flight to Hawaii," Marge replied. "So I hope you brought a book along, I did."

Poppy smiled, and said to Doyle, "I brought one. You can sleep the whole way. You're good at that."

Doyle just gave her a dirty look and sat back. He resigned himself to the fact that if he said something, she'd have a good comeback.

The ride to Metro Airport took about forty minutes, luckily traffic was light. The cab pulled up to their terminal and they took out the luggage.

"Now the part I hate," Doyle said. "The indignity of going through TSA inspections. I made sure I had clean socks on."

"Did you put on clean underwear, too?" Poppy asked Doyle. "They may want to do a cavity search."

Doyle's Paradise

Doyle gave her a look of annoyance. "You can stay here if you want."

They loaded their luggage on a cart and went in the terminal.

One hour later they had gone through the inspection lines and been given a clean appraisal. They sat in stiff chairs as they waited to board the jet. It was sitting out on the tarmac waiting to be boarded.

Finally, the announcement came over the P.A. that they were boarding in order of seating. Doyle looked at his boarding pass and said to Marge, "You didn't get us first class?"

"I was trying to save a little money for you. Besides they can upgrade you once you're on the plane. I'll pull some strings."

"Tell them coach makes me nervous," Doyle said quietly.

They found their seats but then a flight attendant came and led them up front to first class.

"Marge, I'm glad you're with us," Doyle said.

"It's who you know," she joked.

The jet lifted off after getting clearance. Marge was watching out the window as the ground dropped below them quickly. "I love this. I've never been on a plane before. This is going to be a great adventure."

"Have you ever been out of Michigan?" Doyle asked.

"I was in Toledo, Ohio, once when Mac had a police convention to go to. We drove. I explored the city while Mac went to the symposiums and classes. But that was nothing compared to this."

"Well, glad you could come with us," Doyle said. "Now enjoy the flight."

Almost five hours later they flew into the L.A. Airport to switch planes to go to Hawaii.

While in the L.A. terminal, Doyle said, "I called Pacific Island Resort last night and arranged for our stay on the island."

"You didn't tell me that when we were together last night," Poppy said.

"You were in the shower when I called," Doyle said. "I didn't say anything because I wanted to surprise you. I'm sure you worried about where we were going to stay once we were there."

Doyle's Paradise

"I was concerned, but I didn't want to say anything. I figured we'd just camp out on some beach, if we had no accommodations."

"Well, we do, so you can relax," Doyle said as they called for boarding on the Hawaiian flight to the island.

The flight to the main island was a little bumpy, due to a storm over the area. Marge was white knuckling the armrest. Doyle patted her hand and told her to relax.

For what seemed like a long time, the plane was finally coming into the airport in Hawaii, the main island. The storm had passed, but it still could be seen in the distance, like a monster lurking to strike again. They managed to find their luggage and went out to the taxi stands.

One native-looking cabbie came up and said, "Where to, mister?"

"Can you fly us to Pacific Island Resort?" Doyle asked, with a grin.

"No, but I take you to their private airport, pretty quick," he replied in broken English, giving Doyle a toothy smile.

"Lead on," Doyle said and they took their luggage to his cab.

"What do you know about the island?" Doyle asked the driver when they were on the way.

"Pretty nice place, for sure. Lots of palms and lots of sand. Good to be away from civilization."

Poppy grumbled, "And no TV, I suppose."

"Oh, no, Missy. No TV," the driver replied.

"Any radio stations for music?" Marge asked.

"They play music on speakers, good Hawaiian music."

"Delightful," Marge said, less than happy.

"Marge, just for you, I packed an MP3 player with lots of good classic rock on it," Doyle told her.

"Arthur, you are sweet and a lifesaver. I'm all for seclusion, but I still need certain things to make me happy. Music is one and I hope they have coffee."

"I'm sure they will. Now, relax and enjoy yourself," Doyle said.

The cab roared into the small airport at a speed Doyle felt was faster than safe. Everyone was hanging on for their lives.

Doyle's Paradise

"I get you here fast, for sure," the driver said as he got out.

Two men in white jumpsuits approached the car.

"Welcome to Pacific Island Resort," the taller of the two spoke in a dignified voice. "Do you have reservations?"

Doyle fished out a folded sheet of paper from his wild print shirt pocket and handed it to the man. "This came to me through my computer, it's the reservation information."

The man opened the sheet, read, then said, "Excellent, follow me, please. Leave your luggage, we'll get them."

The cab driver was standing, waiting. "Oh, sorry," Doyle said, and pulled out money to pay the man. "If you ever get to the mainland, let me know. I'll get you into the Indy 500."

The driver smiled, jumped back to his car and sped out. Doyle stood watching in wonderment.

"He's never had an accident," the tall man said. "Now, follow me."

They went through glass doors into a lobby dressed up in fake palm trees and murals of the ocean on the walls. It screamed of paradise. They went to a counter where there was a woman in a sarong with a beautiful pair of breasts sticking out dangerously.

"Keep your eyes in, stud," Poppy whispered to him. He laughed and went to the woman.

"Welcome to Pacific Island Resort. We are proud to offer you world class accommodations and recreation. May I have your names?"

Doyle smiled and said, "Arthur Doyle, Poppy Drake, and Marjorie Wayne."

She was looking at the sheet of paper the tall man gave her. "Everything seems to be in order. I'll need to see your credit card to verify it."

Doyle took out his wallet and pulled out the card, handing it to her. She studied it and compared it to the numbers on the sheet, then punched keys on her computer. "Very good, Mr. Doyle. You and your party are now registered. The plane taking you to the island will be ready shortly. We will load your luggage also. If you will follow Victor, he'll take you to the plane."

"Very good, lover boy," Poppy whispered to Doyle as they went out of the lobby. "Your jaw didn't drop when she leaned forward to take your credit card. I think one could see all the way down to her navel."

"I noticed, thank you. I'm a professional and trained not to respond to external stimuli."

"Yes, your stimuli was stimulated. Keep that thought for later in bed," she said with a little blow in his ear.

"You are evil," Doyle said with a grin.

*

Chapter 4

The tall man, now known as Victor, took them to the plane and introduced them to the pilot. Their luggage was already loaded and the pilot said to get in.

The plane had pontoons alongside the wheels and Marge asked nervously, "Is this thing going to land on water?"

"That's the point of pontoons, Marge. We'll be alright," Doyle said, bravely.

"If we drown, I'm coming for you in the afterlife," Poppy threatened.

The pilot could hear their conversation and laughed. "Don't worry. I've flown to the island for years. Never lost a passenger. Well, there was that one time..." he laughed again. "I'm kidding. The nice thing about crashing on the water, the ground hurts more." He laughed again and got in the pilot seat.

His joking didn't help the mood. "This is going to be something to remember," Marge said.

The plane taxied out the runway before taking off. "It'll take about thirty-five minutes to get to the island, so enjoy the ride. All you'll see is water, until we reach the island. Then you'll get off."

"Speaking of getting off, how do we do that?" Doyle asked.

"I taxi right up to a dock and you can climb out. There will be people there who will help take your bags to your room."

"I thought there were no communications to and from the island. How do they know when we are coming?" Doyle asked.

"They have a tall white tower where a little person watches. When he sees me coming, he yells, 'the plane, the plane' and they come out to welcome us." The pilot laughed again.

Doyle's Paradise

"Is this guy high on weed or something?" Poppy asked quietly.

"He is a bit happy, isn't he," Doyle whispered back.

"So you're saying this is like the TV show, *Fantasy Island*?" Marge asked.

"I guess you could say that. Only they don't have a Mr. Roarke. They have a Mr. Dante," the pilot replied.

"Dante, as in the devil?" Poppy asked.

"Dante wasn't the devil, he was a man who enjoyed strolling through the underworld and wrote about it. Hang on, we are coming into Fantasy Island," he said, with another laugh.

The plane banked to the left and they could see the island. It was green and mountainous. They could see inlets and coves and they almost could make out people walking around. The pilot circled one more time and came around for the water landing.

"There's no room on the island for an airstrip, so this is the only way," the pilot said. "Hold on tightly, this can get bumpy."

The plane touched down on the waves and came in for a smooth landing. Doyle breathed easy as did the others. It slowly moved up to the huge dock as men threw out ropes to the pilot who was now standing on one pontoon. They pulled the plane to the dock and tied it off. The pilot opened the door to let the passengers out.

Doyle, Poppy, and Marge came out and stood on the dock, getting their legs, and stomachs back.

"I've been on planes too long today," Marge said. "Good to be finally on land."

A man in a white suit came up to them and said, "Welcome, I'm Mr. Dante, and I'm your host for your stay. Anything you need, anything, let me know."

"How does the pilot know when to pick us up?" Doyle asked.

"Your stay here is only for one week, so he comes back then. Don't worry, we will get you back home safely. Please follow me." He turned and walked up the long dock as they followed him, to a big house at the end of the dock.

In the lobby of the building, they went to a counter where there was another woman in a sarong. Doyle was startled to see it was the same woman as on the mainland. "How did you get out here before us?" Doyle asked.

Doyle's Paradise

The woman grinned and said. "She's my sister, we do look alike. Now I'll assign you your bungalows." She did some typing on her computer and handed them door cards. "In these packets are maps to the island and rules for where you can go and where you can't. Be sure not to wander into areas marked with signs warning that you don't go there."

That piqued Doyle's interest. "That's where they do the experiments on humans," Doyle whispered to Poppy and Marge.

Poppy gave him a dirty look. Marge giggled.

"What about activities?" Marge asked.

"It's all in the packets I'll give you. Take your first night to study it and you'll understand what we have available." She handed out two large folders, adorned with pictures of the island from the air.

A tall man came from out of a hallway and said to follow him. "They have clones on this island," Doyle said seeing the tall man. "Is your name Victor by any chance?" Doyle asked him when they left the building.

The man looked serious, "No, it's Michael. Why?"

"Oh nothing, never mind." Doyle looked at Poppy and said, "They don't have much humor on this island. Other than the pilot."

"Well, you picked this paradise," Poppy responded.

The tall man took them down a path lined with palm trees and ferns. Birds were chirping and making noises along the way. It was very pleasant. They came to two small buildings that were rustic yet modern.

The tall man said, "Your cards will open the locks on the doors. If you have problems with them, let us know."

"Door locks in paradise?" Doyle said. "Do you have crime here?"

The man smiled and said, "No sir. It's just a precaution. They say locks are meant to keep honest people honest. We trust our guests, but we don't do background checks on them. Have a pleasant stay," he said and went off.

"Well, we can go in, I guess. Which bungalow do we get?" Poppy asked.

"Let's see where they put the luggage." Doyle went to the door, pushed his card in and the door clicked open. "I guess I got the right building."

Doyle's Paradise

Marge went to the other building and tried her key, it worked. "I'm glad my bungalow is far enough from yours. In case you get too loud."

"Us, we never get loud. Well, maybe. Poppy tends to make noise," Doyle laughed.

Poppy slapped him and went in the building. "You can sleep outside," she said and closed the door.

"You forget, I have the door key," he called in to her.

"I'm going to get my bags unpacked and take a nap. It's been a long day. Then I'll read the information on the activities around the island. Talk to you later," Marge said, and went in her building.

Doyle stood looking between the two buildings and then turned to see the ocean down the path from them. He took a stroll towards the water and stopped at the beach. The breeze was gentle and warm. The smell of the ocean was invigorating and he felt like taking all his clothes off.

"Don't drown," came a voice behind him. He turned to see Poppy standing there. She came to him and he put his arm around her and pulled her to him.

"No, I was just thinking about getting naked and letting the sun bronze me."

"You'd burn and end up complaining the rest of the week about the pain. Besides you'd sunburn an important part of your body by being naked. So don't do it."

Doyle laughed and said, "I'll protect that part, just for you."

"Good man. Hate to waste a nice vacation," she replied.

*

Chapter 5

They sat on the grass at the edge of the beach, watching the sun slowly dropping into the ocean. It was quiet, other than a few birds singing in the trees. The wind was drifting in easily, and smelled of ocean. The storm had refreshed the air and it still had a little dampness to it.

"I wonder if they get hurricanes out here?" Poppy asked wistfully.

Doyle's Paradise

"All this beauty and solitude around us and you think of hurricanes. Do you also kick little puppies?"

"Only if they get in my way. I think I'll go back to the bungalow and relax, reading about the forbidden places on the island that you will probably go into." She kissed him on the cheek and stood.

He turned his head to watch her go back down the path to the bungalow. He liked watching her from the rear, but the front was nice, too. He was feeling comfortable with her. She tested his mind and his tolerance often. He liked that she could bring out the best in him. He was usually unhappy about life and the way things were going. He felt better since he left the police force and was on his own. But the usual problems, like bills, were always looming. The business was doing better now and the recovery fee they received was a blessing. So Poppy was the cherry on top of the sundae.

He looked back out on the water and could see a boat in the distance. He couldn't tell if it was an ocean going ship or a pleasure craft sailing around the world. He watched until it faded away.

He decided to go in and relax with the instruction booklet of the island. The forbidden areas piqued his curiosity. He didn't think there were any dangerous animals on the island and he hoped they got any snakes removed. So why were there areas that he couldn't go into?

He entered the bungalow and found Poppy asleep in a rattan chair with the papers on her lap. He smiled and picked up the papers and put them on a small table. Then he took her arms and lifted her to the large bed and undressed her carefully, so not to wake her. He covered her with the top sheet and stood admiring her.

She turned her head and said, "Thank you for putting me to bed." Then she grinned.

"How long were you awake?"

"From when you came in the room," she giggled. "I wanted to see what you would do."

"So, how did I do?"

"Very well, now you'll do even better if you crawl in here with me."

Doyle didn't need to be asked twice.

An hour later, Poppy was really asleep and Doyle was seated in the rattan chair. He was reading the booklet about the island and the activities the resort provided. There was typical tourist stuff, tennis, shuffleboard, croquet, cards, chess, and checkers. All things that one could do at home. He wanted to explore the island and enjoy the seclusion.

Doyle's Paradise

In the morning he would see if it was permitted to wander around.

He read about the areas that were off limits to the guests. Mostly it said that there were dangerous sink holes in the ground where one could fall into. That could be a good reason to stay away, he thought. Since there was no cell reception out here, his cell phone was useless for calling for help from a sinkhole. But he would keep it with him, a hard habit to break.

He finally was wearing down. It was a long day and the fun was just beginning, so he crawled into bed. He moved over to Poppy and she was breathing lightly, which comforted him.

The next morning, Poppy was outside as Doyle struggled to get up. Marge came out to greet Poppy and the women talked as Doyle staggered out of the bungalow.

"You look terrible, didn't sleep well?" Marge asked.

"I had dreams of being strapped down and having my head replaced with a dog. Thanks for bringing that up back at the office, Marge," Doyle said, with a slight twist of his head.

"Glad to help," Marge said, with a laugh. "Have you read your instructions for the island?"

"I did," he said. "It's like being on a ship cruise, only no radio communications. I guess the forbidden areas are dangerous to your health from falling into a hole. So I see no reason to venture there. I hope we get to explore, at least."

"What do we do about food?" Poppy asked. "I'd like breakfast."

"Since there is no Wendy's to eat at, the instructions said our meals are served in the big meeting hall back by the docks. It's a buffet and you can eat whatever you can heap on your plate," Doyle said.

"Sure, and the plates are probably five inches across," Poppy said.

"You can pile it on, so you'll make up for it. Let's go see what they have for breakfast." Doyle turned to go back on the path to the main buildings. On the way, they passed a young couple who said a pleasant good morning and passed them by.

"Well, we aren't the only ones here. I haven't seen many people so far," Marge said.

"They're probably all playing shuffleboard," Doyle said with grin.

Doyle's Paradise

They came to the big meeting hall, nicely labeled by a sign and saw other couples moving around the building. They could see the fenced in courts tennis and the area for the shuffleboard courts. There were two couples taking advantage of playing tennis.

"They could play tennis back in civilization. They should be exploring or running nude on the beaches," Doyle said.

"You just want to watch naked women running around," Poppy scolded.

"Sure, and you wouldn't watch the men?" he shot back.

They went in the meeting hall and found it decorated with lots of island greenery and huge murals of water scenes. There was a long table set up with all kinds of food and there were four couples taking advantage. The room had a dozen individual tables, with seating for four and a couple for six. Poppy made a bee-line to the food, with Doyle and Marge following.

"There you go, the plates are huge," Doyle told Poppy. "For what I'm paying, they better be huge."

"I don't want to know how much this week is costing. I just want to think we're lost on an island after a shipwreck," she replied.

"May as well be," Doyle said as he put pancakes and sausages on his plate. He usually didn't eat breakfast, but the sea air made him hungry.

They went to a table and were greeted by other guests on the way. Everyone seemed overly friendly.

"Do you think they're Stepford robots?" Doyle asked. "They're way too friendly."

"They're just happy to be in paradise. Stop grumbling," she chastised him.

They looked up to see Mr. Dante standing by the table.

"And how are our new guests today?" he asked pleasantly.

"We're doing well, so far. Once we explore, we'll be better," Doyle answered. "Just how many people are guests at this time?"

"We presently have forty people on the island. You are the last to be brought on for now. We only allow forty to be registered at one time. Otherwise someone would have to sleep on the beach," he said with a wide smile.

Doyle smiled back and said, "I wouldn't mind that."

Chapter 6

"I'm glad you enjoy roughing it, Mr. Doyle. Most men who come here aren't very happy to be away from their televisions and sports. It's their wives, or girlfriends who talk them into coming. We try to make their stay as pleasant as possible," Dante said, still showing his wide smile.

"Do you ever have any problems serious enough to warrant communications back to civilization?" Doyle asked.

"No, Mr. Doyle. All the staff in our employ are trained to handle any situation that may come up, short of a hurricane," he replied, still holding his smile. Doyle thought he may have had cosmetic surgery to freeze it in place. "We feel that the seclusion and lack of dependency on the main island is our goal. Excuse me, I have duties to attend to. Enjoy your stay." He went off, briskly.

"Hurricane?" Poppy repeated. "I told you they have hurricanes."

"I don't remember hearing anything about a hurricane in the near future. That's something they keep track of," Doyle replied.

"The food is very good," Marge said between bites, changing the subject. "I think they use natural ingredients, and not boxed foods."

Doyle took in the last of his sausages and agreed. "So, what do we want to do today? I'm not playing tennis, or croquet."

"From what I read, the only things you can do here are wandering about and enjoying the beaches. There's no tour that takes you around to see the sights. They don't even have a volcano to jump into," Poppy said, trying not to laugh.

"Okay, so it's a little boring," Doyle admitted. "Let's just try to make the best of it. We're here for the week, until the plane comes back to get us. The idea was to get away from stress and just relax. I read that they do have a small library, so we can read books on the beach."

"Yes, and you don't like to swim, I presume?" Poppy asked.

"No, I like to swim, just not with sharks. They have inland lagoons that are safe to swim in," he said finishing his meal.

Marge was still enjoying her food. She had heaped her plate with a little of everything and was taking her time eating. "Why don't you two go for a walk and see what trouble you can get into? I'm

41

going to relax here with all this delicious food, then go back and get my book to read, or maybe knit in the sunshine."

"I wouldn't want to leave you alone Marge," Doyle said.

"Nonsense, you two need to be alone with each other. Now go and enjoy. I'm fine here and I'm a big girl, so I can take care of myself. Go," she said, still eating.

Doyle looked at Poppy and stood, "You heard the lady, go." He helped her up and they went to the exit. Doyle stopped just inside the door when he saw a notice on the wall. He read it and said, "They have a small band that plays here nights for dancing under the stars. Sounds like a good deal."

"I can go for that. It's sounding a little better now," she replied.

They went out and headed down a path that had a sign saying it was a nature trail. "Shall we go check out the nature?"

Poppy took his hand and said, "Fine with me."

The nature trail twisted through the jungle setting, every so often there was a metal plaque on a pole explaining what the exotic plant or tree was behind it.

They walked a little further when they heard a terrifying scream from ahead. They ran to find a woman off the path holding her hands over her mouth. She turned to them as they ran up, trying to talk, but nothing was coming out but gasps.

"Take your time, and a big breath." Doyle waited a couple seconds as she gasped for air. "What happened to scare you?" he asked expecting to hear she stepped on a snake.

She was still gasping and then pointed off the trail. Doyle looked in the direction and could see a person on the ground in the dense brush. "Wait here," he said and went to the person. It was a man lying on the ground, looking dead. He leaned down and touched the man's neck to check for a pulse, he found none. He turned the man slightly and saw the bullet hole in his chest. He set the man back down.

He returned to the woman and asked, "What happened?"

She was more composed now and said between breaths, "We were playing around, hide and seek. I came up the path and looked around. I saw him on the ground, I thought he was hiding and went to him. I know enough about bodies to tell he was dead. That's when I screamed. Thank you for coming."

"You heard nothing, no gun shots?"

43

Doyle's Paradise

"Gun shots? He was shot? I heard nothing but birds. How could he be shot without me hearing it? I wasn't that far back."

"I don't know, but we need to get the staff out here to take the body back to the compound," he said and looked at Poppy. "Wait here with her, and I'll run to get help."

Poppy agreed and Doyle ran off down the trail until he broke out into a clearing by the main offices. Mr. Dante was standing on the porch talking to another man. Doyle ran to them.

"Mr. Dante, we have a problem. There's a man on the trail and he's dead. It looks like a gunshot. I'll take you there, you'll need a stretcher," Doyle said, between gulps of breath.

Dante told the man to get some other men and the doctor. Doyle waited as they scurried around, getting ready to go. Doyle led them back to where the body was. Poppy was holding the woman as she was still crying.

Doyle pointed into the brush and three men went in with the stretcher. The doctor, with his bag, stood on the trail waiting for them to come out.

"Back in civilization, it wouldn't be right to disturb the crime scene, but I guess this is an

44

exception," Doyle said to the doctor. "You'll find the man was shot, but the woman said she didn't hear the shot. When you remove the bullet, I may know if it was from a handgun or rifle. The hole was small, so I'd say it was a .22."

"You seem to know something about crime scenes," the doctor said.

"I was a homicide detective for the Detroit Police, retired, and I'm now working as a private investigator. I've seen my share of crime scenes."

"How did you come upon this?"

"My girlfriend and I were taking the nature trail when we heard the woman scream," he said as the men brought out the body on the stretcher, placing it on the trail.

The doctor went to the body and looked it over. He studied the bullet hole for a moment and said, "Yes, it does look like a .22, small enough. I'll remove it and you can examine it in my office, Mr..." he paused.

"Doyle, Art Doyle. Thanks, I'll wait."

"I'm not really set up to do an autopsy, but I think we know what happened."

Mr. Dante came walking up and looked startled by the body. Doyle noticed the smile was now gone. "What happened?" Dante asked.

"Looks like you may have a killer in paradise," Doyle replied.

*

Chapter 7

Poppy helped the woman back to the offices where they took the body. The doctor had a small building off to the side where the clinic was for emergencies or illness. They took the man into a room with a table and transferred the body from the stretcher to the table. The men left the room, leaving the doctor, Mr. Dante and Doyle alone.

Poppy said she'd stay with the woman, now identified as Lorna Kabe, in the waiting room. The man was identified as Elmer Kabe, her husband. They had been on the island for two days and were newlyweds. This disturbed Doyle, as they shouldn't have suffered a violent death on their honeymoon.

The doctor, Walter Hakon, took out his instruments and proceeded to dig for the bullet. After a bit of fighting for the tiny object, he came out with it and put it on a tray.

Doyle moved closer to it and said, "Yep, it's a .22, but I can't tell if it's from a handgun or from a rifle. I'd say he was murdered with a rifle. Kabe could have been shot from a long distance, which is why his wife didn't hear the sound." He turned to Dante and asked, "Do you have a shooting range on the island?"

"No, Mr. Doyle, we don't approve of guns on the island," he replied.

"Well, you don't check close enough for weapons," Doyle said and took his Sig Sauer from its belt holster under his shirt.

Dante looked shocked. "Mr. Doyle, why do you have a gun?"

"Mr. Dante, I'm a private investigator, former FBI agent, and former Detroit homicide detective. I'm permitted to carry. I never leave home without it. And I think if you have a killer on the island, it may help to have some protection."

"We have security men in case of problems," he defended.

"Are they armed?"

"Well, no. But they do have rifles locked in the main office."

"That's a good place to start. Take me to your arsenal. Let's eliminate that this shot came from one of your weapons."

Dante looked confused then said, "Yes, of course. Follow me."

Doyle told the doctor to lock up the bullet and followed Dante.

Doyle told Poppy, as he passed, that he would be back. The two men went around to the main office and into a room marked "Security". There was a man in jungle khakis sitting at a desk. He sported a brush cut, looking to be in his early thirties, with a bit of extra weight on his body. Probably Dante's nephew, Doyle thought.

"Morris, we need to see the rifles. This is Mr. Doyle, he's investigating a murder. Mr. Doyle, this is Albert Morris, head of our security," Dante said.

"A murder? On the island? When?" Morris asked.

"In the last hour, now take us to the rifles."

Morris stood and took the men into what amounted to a closet. The rifles were locked in a wall mount rack and Norris took out a key. He stood back as Doyle went and checked each of the five rifles on the wall.

"Okay, none of these have been fired recently. Any other weapons that your team may have?" Doyle asked the man.

"Not that I'm aware of. We have a strict policy about weapons on the island."

Doyle pulled the Sig again and said, "You should have put that in the brochure." Morris looked stunned as Doyle put the gun back and turned to Dante standing just outside of the room.

"Someone else didn't get the message about the ban on weapons. Kabe was shot from what I believe was a rifle. Kind of hard to smuggle on the island. Unless it breaks down, like one a professional killer would have. They're easy to put in luggage."

"Do you think this could have been a professional hit on the man?" Dante asked.

"If someone had a hit on the man, this is not the best place to do it. No way to escape from being found. The killer is still on the island and the sooner we talk to the guests, the sooner we can eliminate the innocent."

Doyle's Paradise

Morris looked annoyed and asked, "What makes you qualified to handle this?"

"Albert - it is Albert, right? I've been in law enforcement for over thirty years. I was in the FBI chasing terrorists, probably when you were in elementary school, then with the Detroit police as a homicide detective. I'm now a private investigator in Detroit. So, what's your background?"

Morris stood, looking dumb. "Just a security guard in San Francisco, so I guess you have me beat."

"Let's not be pissy over this, we have to work together to find this person before he possibly kills again. How many men do you have in your team?"

"Four," Morris replied. "Two on twelve hour shifts then the others take over for twelve."

"Well, they're going to be working overtime. Roust them out, we have to talk to the guests and find out where they all were."

Morris left the room as Doyle asked Dante, "Can you get every one of the forty guests, minus one now, in the meeting room so we can talk?"

"I'll have the staff round up everyone."

"To be on the safe side, have all your staff present also, so we can talk to them."

"You don't think one of my people could have done this?"

"I suspect everyone, until I find they have an alibi. Now get those people moving," Doyle said and went out of the security room. He went back to the clinic and found Poppy sitting next to Mrs. Kabe, who was asleep on the couch.

"The doctor gave her a sedative, so she could rest. What's up?"

"Dante is gathering all the guests so we can talk to them. Since you're an insurance investigator, you should be able to interrogate people."

"Should I use a rubber hose to beat the truth out of them?"

"No, but you can pull their finger nails out if you want."

Poppy kissed Doyle. "I like the way you think. Now, shall we go interrogate people?"

"First, I have to talk to the doctor about the body. Wait here." He went into the room where Kabe was still resting on the table. The doctor was putting a jar containing the bullet in a cabinet and turned to see Doyle enter.

Doyle's Paradise

"What are you going to do with the body? I presume you don't have a morgue here?"

"I'm concerned about that. He should be put in a cold place, but all we have are cold lockers for food and I don't think people will like having a dead body next to their sides of beef."

"Can we wrap him up in plastic and put him in the back of the cold storage?"

"That probably would be the best solution. I'll take care of it, you have to go catch a killer."

"Thanks, Doc. I'll be back." Doyle left the room and took Poppy to the meeting hall. Doyle did a quick count and there were about twenty-nine people in the room. More were coming shortly after. Everyone looked either concerned, confused or annoyed.

Doyle stood on the small stage up front where they had the band equipment set up. "People, may I have your attention?" he called out. The guests turned their attentions to him. "Everyone please find a seat and relax, I'll explain shortly why we are gathering here."

They waited another twenty minutes as more people came in. The staff was asking them to have a seat. Dante came up to Doyle. "I think they are all here, unless you want to take a roster count?"

"I counted thirty-six people, minus Kabe, his wife, my girlfriend and myself. That's forty unless you overbooked?"

"No, Mr. Doyle, there were only forty guests." Dante finally cracked a smile.

"Are all your staff here?"

"Yes, I made sure. Other than the wife and the doctor, he's busy with the body."

"Good, let's start finding our killer."

*

Chapter 8

Doyle went to Poppy and said, "Do me a favor, go back to Mrs. Kabe, wake her if you have to. Ask her everything she knows about her husband. Job, friends, background, anything she knows. Write it down and bring it to me." Poppy agreed and went out of the building.

Doyle went to the stage again. "All right, listen up and be quiet." He waited until they quieted down. "Okay, we have a situation that requires us to ask you questions. There has been a death on the island and we need to find out where everyone was within the last two hours. Please be patient and we'll get to you. Thanks." He stepped off the stage and was going to talk to Morris.

Some man in the group yelled, "Is this a police investigation?"

Doyle stopped and turned to the group. "Who asked that?" he yelled. Finally a man held his hand up. "Are you by chance a lawyer or a criminal?"

The man quietly said lawyer. Doyle went to him. "Well, Mr. Lawyer, you will be the first person I'll question."

"Are you the police?" he asked.

"No, I'm the man who will kick your ass if you don't cooperate. I'm a private investigator, as close to real police as you'll get on this island. By the way…" Doyle turned to Dante. "Mr. Dante, this island is in international waters, correct?"

Dante said it was. Doyle turned back to the man. "So you have no say here, Mr. Lawyer. Now get up and follow me, before I get pissed."

Doyle went back to the door as the man sheepishly followed. He stopped at the door and told the man to stay there. Morris was guarding the door and Doyle told him to have his men talk to everyone and find out what they were doing when the murder was committed between two and two-thirty, and to write down names and alibis. Morris said he'd take care of it.

Doyle pointed to the lawyer and told him to follow. They went outside and Doyle turned to him. "Other than being a wiseass, you may be able to help. As a lawyer you understand all the ins and outs of criminal behavior, right?" The man agreed. "Good, I'll need your help later to find a killer. One of the people in this building murdered a guest about two hours ago. We need to find out where everyone was and who may have motive. That's when I'll need you. So hang in there and behave. Go back and sit down, but don't say anything. By the way, what's your name?"

"Terrence White," he replied.

"I'm Doyle, pleasure to meet you, even though you're a lawyer. I don't like lawyers, so don't piss me off." Doyle held the door open for him and he went in. Doyle saw Poppy coming from the clinic and he waited.

"I talked to the wife and found out a number of interesting things about her husband. Want to talk about them now?" Poppy said.

Doyle's Paradise

"May as well, we're not going anywhere fast. What did you find out?"

"Kabe was an attorney for some big company in New York, the wife didn't know the name. She thinks the company may have been connected with the mob. At least that's the opinion she got from brief conversations she had with her husband. He was very secretive about his job, but he told her to go to her parents in Florida if anything happened to him. I don't think if the company was reputable, he would be concerned about his life."

"The shooting looked like a pro hit, but I don't understand why it was done here. The killer has no way to get off the island, unless he has a submarine off shore." Doyle thought about this new information. "If Kabe had mob connections, it may be why he was killed."

"I thought there were only couples on the island? Other than Marge."

"Maybe the hit man brought his wife for a little pleasure and a little business," Doyle said with a grin. "We may have a husband and wife hit team,"

"Why not, we're a boyfriend and girlfriend investigating team. Maybe we could get married and form a real team," Poppy said with a smirk.

"Let's not rush into that. Anything else on him?"

"Just standard stuff, he seemed to lead a normal life other than his work. The wife didn't really know much about him. They only met a year ago and just now married."

"So, no children, I presume."

"None. She has to start over."

"I suppose as an insurance investigator, you asked if he had a life insurance policy?"

"He did, but it was in his parents' names as beneficiaries. He wasn't going to change it yet until they married."

"What does she do for a living?"

"She's a secretary at a mortgage firm. She makes a lousy wage, she said."

"So, she's basically broke. Shame. Let's go in and see what everyone is saying about where they were."

They went in the building and stood by the door. Doyle could see that Morris had done a good job of breaking the guests into four groups so his men could talk to them. He hoped they were smart enough to ask the right questions.

Doyle's Paradise

Dante came over to them and asked, "What are you going to do now?"

"I'll be talking to your security men to see what they found, then I'll be asking more questions." Doyle looked over to the side and saw Marge sitting by herself. He turned to Poppy and asked her to give Marge some company. Poppy went over to the woman and sat down.

Morris came over and said, "We're about done talking to the people. From what I gather, everyone was with other people at the time of the murder. No one was alone in the last couple hours that we could find."

"Thanks, Albert. I still want to talk to them individually. So keep them together."

About twenty minutes later, Morris' men had finished and were telling Doyle what they found. Doyle was glad the men seemed responsible enough to ask the right questions.

"Make me a list of those people who may have had shaky alibis. I'll start talking to them."

Morris took the men off to the side to a table and had them make their lists. Doyle excused himself from Dante and went to Marge and Poppy.

Bob Moats

"Arthur, do you think one of these people could have murdered the man?" Marge asked.

"Unless there's someone else on this island that we don't know about, I'd say it was a good bet. Come with me, the two of you." He led the women to a small round table by the stage and had them sit. "I'm going to be questioning people and I want you two to listen in. Poppy, you've dealt with insurance fraud cheats enough to tell who may be hiding something, so jump in whenever you feel the need." She agreed.

Doyle went back up on the stage and called out. "May I have your attention, please?" He waited, then when the room was quiet, he continued. "The island security team asked basic questions as to where everyone was during the last two to three hours. Around two-fifteen, a man was shot by an unknown assailant and we need to find that person. My name is Doyle, I was with the FBI in their terrorist tactical force and most recently a Detroit Police homicide detective. I'm now a private investigator and I intend to find the killer of Elmer Kabe. Now you know who I am, I'll need to get to know you a little better. So if you can be patient a little longer, I'll get to everyone as quickly as possible."

*

Chapter 9

Doyle stepped off the stage and pointed to Terrence White, the lawyer. "Why don't you come over here and talk, Mr. Lawyer?"

White stood and made his way through the people all sitting quietly at the tables. He approached the table where Marge, Poppy, and now Doyle, sat.

"Have a seat, White," Doyle said pointing to the chair across the table from them. "First, let me introduce you to Poppy Drake, insurance investigator, and my secretary Marjorie Wayne. I call her Marge, but you can call her Mrs. Wayne." Doyle smiled, sat back and asked, "Where are you a lawyer at?"

"Meriman, Halper and Gotleib. In Houston, Texas," he replied, stiffly.

"Relax, White. I don't bite. Unless it's needed. Did you know Elmer Kabe?"

"No, can't say as I do. Is he the victim?"

"He is. Shot in the jungle by an unknown assailant. I think it was from a high powered rifle from a distance. His wife was nearby and didn't hear the gunshot."

"Could be a silencer on a handgun," White replied.

"Anything is possible. What were you doing around two-fifteen?"

White was running his memory back to the time and said, "I was with my wife and another couple having drinks by the tennis courts. We had used up our time on the court and were relaxing, while another couple used the court."

"Since you didn't know Kabe, then you couldn't know what he did for a living."

"No, I couldn't."

"He was a lawyer, in New York. His wife thinks the company he worked for was connected to organized crime. You don't know any companies in New York that fit that description, by chance?"

"I have no connections to New York, so I wouldn't know. Do you think this could be a hit on the man?"

"We're investigating that line. Unfortunately, since we are cut off from the rest of the world, I can't find out much more than what his wife tells us. She doesn't have much to tell, since her husband was fairly secretive about his job. I plan on questioning her when she's feeling a little better."

Poppy asked, "What kind of law do you practice?"

"Corporate law. We represent a number of big building companies in Houston that deal with contractors and they need us to work out the contracts."

"There's no organized crime in Houston?" Poppy asked.

"There is everywhere, Ms. Drake. In Houston there is a lot of construction. We have to keep the contractors in line so no one gets screwed. Lots of money in these buildings being put up."

Doyle sat forward, "Can you go get the people you were having drinks with, and bring them here, please."

"Sure," White said and stood. He went to the guests and talked to one man. They said something to their wives and everyone got up, heading over to Doyle. Doyle came around the table and stopped them before they arrived. He looked to the new man and brought him to the table, leaving the three others behind.

"Your name?" Doyle asked.

"Mickey Jaffarie," he replied.

"Just a quick question. Were you with these people around two-fifteen by the tennis court?" Doyle pointed to White, his wife, and Jaffarie's wife.

He thought and said, "I was, or I should say we were. Our time on the court ended at two and then we sat to have drinks. We were there at least an hour or more."

"I could check the tennis court log to verify that you were on the court at that time," Doyle asked.

"Sure, they keep track of the time. They even have a line judge who can verify we were there at that time."

"Very good, follow me." He took Jaffarie back to his friends. "White, I may still need you to help later. I just wanted to verify your alibi," Doyle said. "Now all four of you can leave the building and go enjoy your vacation," he smiled, and then said ominously, "Just don't get shot." He turned away from them and went over to the other guests still waiting. White and Jafferie looked at each other with surprised expressions. They left the room quickly.

For the next hour and a half, Doyle and Poppy questioned the guests and found that everyone had an alibi. The room was empty now of guests and staff. Dante went off to take care of island business and Morris was getting his men back to work.

"I didn't sense any deceit in their answers," Poppy said.

"I didn't either," Doyle replied. "So do we have a hidden person on the island or is one of these people very clever with his or her lies? In all my years of interrogating people, I've met a number of pathological liars. Very good at telling their story and making it sound logical. But they always slip up eventually and give themselves away. So I guess we just observe the guests and watch what they do. Maybe we'll make someone nervous and they'll screw up. I'd like to talk to the wife now."

Marge said she was going back to her bungalow and rest. Doyle asked Morris if he could have one of his men escort Marge to her bungalow. Doyle and Poppy went back to the clinic and found the wife sitting on the couch, looking upset. Doyle sat on the coffee table in front of her as Poppy sat next to her.

"Mrs. Kabe, I'm very sorry for your loss, but in order for us to find the killer, I need some more information."

"I understand, Mr. Doyle. Ask what you need to find this bastard. I want to see him strung up. I'm a newlywed, for crying out loud. My husband was murdered before we could even start a life." She started to tear up. Poppy took a couple tissues from the box next to the couch and handed them to her. "Thank you. What do you need to know?"

"Tell me about your husband."

"Where should I start?"

"How about when you met?"

"We met through friends. I was just getting over a bad romance when my friends set me up with Elmer. I wasn't happy about it and I think he knew. I wasn't very nice. He was. I started to relax with him and by the end of the night we agreed to meet again. After eight months of dating he proposed. I was shocked. He had a good job, or so he said, so I figured he could provide for me. I never questioned his work. He said he was a lawyer and worked for a big company that handled sales of industrial equipment and supplies. They also had connections to waste disposal, you know, trash pickup. I had always heard that the mob had connections to trash companies, so I started to assume the company was mob related."

"But he never said they were?"

"No, he would get annoyed if I questioned him about it. I didn't like worrying about his life, if someone would have a problem with him."

"Why might you think this shooting has to do with his job?"

"I have no idea. He never talked about it, so I don't know what he was involved in."

Doyle paused, giving her time to relax. "Mrs. Kabe, I hate to ask, but may I examine your husband's belongings? Maybe I'll find something he was murdered for."

"You can take all his things. I don't have much use for them now, do I?" She wiped her eyes, took a big breath and sat back on the couch.

*

Chapter 10

"I have to ask, what were you and Elmer doing in the jungle, when he was murdered?" Doyle asked.

"I thought I told you in the jungle? We were messing around, playing hide and seek. He went off as I stood waiting with my eyes closed. I counted to fifty and then went looking. I walked down the trail a little ways and then I saw him just off the trail, lying on the ground. I went to him and since I took a first aid class in college, I could tell he was dead. That's when I screamed. You two came rushing up, and you know the rest."

"You heard no gunshots at all?"

"No, nothing."

"What kind of noises were there at the time?"

"Mostly birds, but I could hear the ocean on the shore near the trail. It was making such a pretty sound lapping on the shore." She paused, then continued, "While I had my eyes closed, I thought I heard a jet overhead. It had to be up high because the sound was faint. Years ago in New York, I lived near an airport and could hear the jets all day. There were no sounds other than what I told you, so nothing to hide a gunshot."

"That's fine. Relax and after I talk to the doctor, we'll go and look at Elmer's things." Doyle stood leaving Poppy and Kabe. He went into the room where the body had been held earlier. The doctor was washing his hands as Doyle entered.

"Mr. Doyle, I just had Morris' men take Kabe to the meat locker. I wrapped him in disposable bags and tightly duct taped it closed. I hope he stays fresh for some mainland ME to examine."

Doyle's Paradise

"We're out in international waters, but I'm sure the Honolulu PD will take him in. Hang on to the bullet, so they can examine it. I really hate being cut off from civilization. It's frustrating."

"I felt that way when I first came out here to work. I was worried that if some really serious accident occurred, would I be able to handle it? The worse thing to happen, other than this murder, was a cut leg from some woman climbing a rock. I've gotten used to the seclusion."

"I like the big city life, although I have a cabin in the woods back in Michigan. I like to go there to relax. But I have the option to hit a couple bars if I feel the need," Doyle smiled.

"Our bar here is well stocked and we have able bartenders, the ambiance is nice and peaceful."

"No bar fights?" Doyle asked with a grin.

"Oh, sure, we've had a few. Our security handles it quickly and discreetly. No real serious knock down drag out fights."

"Good. So the body will go back on the next plane. When will that be?"

"There's a bunch of guests ready to leave the day before you do. So they'll have to share the ride."

"How often do they rotate guests?" Doyle asked.

"Dante likes to have them come out in groups, so the plane doesn't have to come back as often. You and your friends were an exception. You came out the day after this group arrived."

"I noticed the plane could hold about forty people. So they go back, then you bring in another group?"

"Yep, easy in, easy out. Each stay on the island is only one week. Never more than forty at one time. You and your friends made up the forty for this trip."

"I think the body should go back with me. Not a good idea to have a dead man on a plane with thirty-seven guests." Doyle paused then said, "Thirty-eight guests? With myself, my girlfriend and my secretary, that makes forty-one."

"I guess Dante made an exception this time. He likes to keep it simple, but will bend the rules occasionally."

"Well, thanks for your help. I'll check in to be sure they don't accidently serve our dead man for supper."

The doctor laughed and said, "I made sure to inform the kitchen staff to leave him alone."

Doyle's Paradise

Doyle saluted the doctor and went back to the women. "Shall we go?"

They followed Mrs. Kabe to her bungalow and went in. She pointed to her late husband's luggage and said, "Do what you have to. I'd feel better if it was all taken out. Nothing I want to see to remember him by."

Doyle went to the bags on the bed and opened them. He saw a briefcase on the floor and asked if it was his. She said it was. He lifted it to the bed and tried to open it, but it was locked.

"Do you have a key for this?" Doyle asked.

"No, I don't know where he would keep it. I'll get his keys, it must be with them." She went to a desk and moved some clothes, bringing up a set of keys. She gave them to Doyle and he went through them to find the one that would open the briefcase. The case contained papers, lots of them. There was a calculator and something that surprised him. It was a satellite phone.

"Mrs. Kabe, do you know why your husband had a satellite phone?" Doyle asked.

"I know he had one, but didn't know he brought it. He would sometimes take trips outside the United States, and it kept him connected."

"Well, he must have needed to be connected here. I'm sure he didn't tell anyone he had it. This really changes things." He looked at Poppy. "I think we'll keep this to ourselves for a while. It may come in handy."

"Why would he need to be connected? What was so important that he couldn't leave it home?" Poppy asked.

Doyle looked at Mrs. Kabe. "Did your husband have some kind of deals to make for his company?"

"I wish I could tell you, but I don't know. He never discussed business with me," she said.

"I'm going to take this case back to my bungalow and study the contents. Maybe I'll find something to help."

"Take it all," Mrs. Kabe said. "I have to start over."

She looked ill, so Poppy said to Doyle, "Let's leave Mrs. Kabe to rest. I'll help carry this stuff to our place."

"Thank you Mrs. Kabe," Doyle said.

"Please call me Lorna. I don't want to use Mrs. Kabe now."

"Sure, Lorna. You rest and we'll talk later." Doyle and Poppy gathered the bags and went out.

"She sure is leaving her husband behind. Seems strange she doesn't want to hang on to his memory," Poppy said.

"Not everyone is sentimental. Some people just want to get over bad times and move on," Doyle replied.

"Would you get over me if I left you?"

"In a flash, and on to another woman," Doyle said, with a big grin.

"You're lucky I'm holding luggage, or I'd hit you."

They got back to their bungalow and found Marge on her porch with her knitting. She waved to them. They took the luggage in the building and went back out to Marge.

"So, what's happening?" Marge asked as they came up to her porch.

"We have an interesting development. One that will connect us to civilization."

Chapter 11

"Oh, how will you do that?" Marge asked.

"It seems Kabe had a satellite phone with him. If it works, I can contact Oscar back in New York. He may be able to help me sort things out on Kabe's job in New York."

"A satellite phone? Can it actually reach to a satellite?" Marge asked with wonderment.

Doyle laughed gently, not wanting to offend Marge's wide-eyed amazement. "It does, and it will help to reach the mainland. I have to find out what Kabe was up to now that I have his briefcase and his papers. I hope it sheds some light on this."

"It would be nice to wrap this up for the widow. You didn't seem to have any luck with the guests," Marge observed.

"Yeah, and I'm still not sure what happened. I don't even have an inkling as to who may have done it." He looked at Poppy, "It's getting late, long day and I want to dig into the briefcase, so shall we retire to our island bungalow and ferret out a killer?"

"Lead the way," Poppy said, then, "Later, Marge, maybe I'll come over and we can go watch the sun go down in the ocean."

"That would be nice, if you can." Marge went back to her knitting, as Doyle and Poppy went back to their bungalow.

"I'm really excited that Kabe brought his phone with him. Not that I'm happy we found it this way, but it evens things up," Doyle said as he put the briefcase on the desk.

"You can investigate. I'm taking a quick forty-winks of sleep. Wake me if you find the killer." She smiled and went to the bed and collapsed. Doyle watched her lying on the bed with her beautiful legs stretched out. He had to keep his mind on the objective.

"Oh, hell," he said and went to the bed and crawled in next to her.

"What's up, sailor? Are you in port for a little fun?" she asked.

"Anchors away," he muttered and started nuzzling her neck.

An hour later, the two got up and re-dressed. Poppy said, "Well, that was fun. Next time you're in port, look me up."

Doyle laughed, went to the briefcase and sat at the desk. He flipped the latches and opened the case. He lifted a number of papers out and set them on the desk, then he started to sort through them.

"Seems to be a lot of legal papers, contracts and proposals for building contractors. Nothing out of the ordinary, just stuff a lawyer would understand. I may need Terrence White to help sort through this."

"Do you want me to go find him and bring him here? It's still early," Poppy asked.

"Would you? I really think that would help."

"I'll be right back, if I have to drag him." Poppy went out, and Doyle went back to the papers. They were all foreign to him, full of legalese and double talk. No wonder lawyers get paid well, he thought.

Doyle put the satellite phone in his suitcase, to hide it. He made sure it was shut off.

About twenty minutes later, Poppy returned with White. "Terrence, or can I call you Terry?" Doyle asked.

"You can," he replied.

Doyle's Paradise

"Well, Terry, I have a situation. Our dead man was an attorney for some company called New York Heavy Equipment and Sales. I gathered that from his papers, but I can't make much out of this mess. Can you look at the papers and maybe tell me what they were up to?"

"If you think it will help, sure," White replied.

Doyle pulled over a second chair next to the desk and handed White a stack of papers. White flipped through the stack and took time reading. He got up and went to the bed, putting papers in separate piles. "You don't mind, do you?" he asked.

"No, do what you have to."

White sorted through more papers from the briefcase and said, "This Kabe wasn't very organized, or he grabbed a lot of contracts, billings and briefs quickly, without sorting them. Almost like he was cleaning out his desk and taking things with him." White continued to sort each pile into smaller piles.

"Well, Doyle, if I'm reading this right, there was a lot of collusion going on in his company. Double billings for services and supplies. I'm wondering if half of these companies they deal with are even real."

"How does the company make money off double billing?"

"They don't. It's all bookkeeping for tax purposes. They fake bills and use those for write-offs. Lots of companies do it, most don't get caught. This company had lots of dealings and most look to have been faked. That's my opinion."

"Okay, would Kabe be in trouble if he was bringing this to the attention of the law?"

"I don't think his bosses would like it. Just a quick accounting of what I saw, this is millions of dollars in sales that were items sold to different companies, but there weren't enough supplies to fulfill the sales. That's why I think the companies were faked. Kabe kept documentation of what went on in his company. That's all in this pile here. This is the most damaging of the papers."

Doyle sat mulling over what he heard. "If his bosses sent someone to hit Kabe, they'd want these papers back wouldn't they?"

"This is damaging evidence. They surely would want this stuff back," White said.

Doyle looked at Poppy. "If they murdered Kabe, then they aren't finished with the objective. That means Lorna could be in danger if the hitman goes after these papers, thinking she still has them."

"Damn," Poppy uttered. "I'll go check on her. You should hide this stuff." Poppy stood and went out the door.

Doyle picked up the damning pile and put it in his suitcase. He turned to White and said, "Thanks, now you need to get away from us, so you aren't associated with this."

"No problem, I don't know you and I'm out of here." He turned and went out the door.

Doyle packed the papers back into the briefcase and closed it up. He went out the door and over to Lorna's bungalow. The door was open and he went up to it cautiously drawing his Sig from its holster.

"Poppy?" he called out. He heard nothing and went in the doorway with his gun out front. "Poppy?" he called again. He heard his name called out from the outside and he rushed out. "Poppy," he yelled loudly now.

"Doyle, I'm down here," Poppy replied from a distance. Doyle went in the direction of the sound, heading down the path toward the beach. He came out of the bush and found Poppy standing over Lorna, sitting on the sand, crying. He put his gun back in the holster and went to her.

"Is she all right?" Doyle asked.

Poppy pulled Doyle away from her. "It's catching up to her now. The reality is rearing its ugly head. I'm letting her cry it out and then we'll keep an eye on her."

"No one approached her about her husband?"

"No, she was able to tell me that she wasn't bothered by anyone," Poppy replied.

"Maybe we need to put her in with Marge for tonight, until I can talk with Morris and see if he can provide her with protection."

"That might be a good idea. You go talk to Marge and I'll get Lorna settled here first, before we come."

"Good. Do you have your gun?'

Poppy lifted her blouse and showed him her .38 caliber handgun in its holster. "If Dante knew we both had guns, he might be upset."

"He'll get over it. We need to catch this killer and since he has a weapon, we need to be equalized."

"If this guy has a rifle, should we be out in the open?" Poppy asked, looking around.

Doyle thought on that and said, "Very true, let's get moving." Doyle went back to talk to Marge and Poppy helped Lorna up from the sand.

"Of course, Arthur. Bring her here and she can stay over," Marge said when Doyle explained.

Poppy came up the path with Lorna and went over to Marge.

"Thank you, Mrs. Wayne. I appreciate you letting me stay with you. Poppy explained the danger I may be in."

"No one will harm you, dear," Marge said and reached in her knitting bag and brought out her .357 magnum. "No one."

*

Chapter 12

"Marge, you amaze me," Doyle exclaimed. "I didn't know you brought your gun."

"I never leave home without it. And it's loaded this time," Marge said with a very wide smile. "Now, Lorna, shall we get you settled in the bungalow?" She stood and took the woman into her building.

"Okay that settles that," Doyle said. "Now, if this hit man knew who Kabe was, he had to know his wife and where they were staying. I think I may camp out in the Kabe bungalow tonight in case of visitors. Feel like a camp out?"

"Shall we pitch a tent?" Poppy smiled.

"Let's go there carefully. We don't know if the hit man is watching. Hell, he may have seen us bring Lorna here. Maybe you should camp out here tonight."

Poppy thought about it and said, "I think that's a good idea. We girls can have a pajama party. I'll tell Marge." Poppy went in the bungalow as Doyle went back to his building. He took the briefcase and went over to the Kabe bungalow with it. He set it on the desk and went over to the rattan chair and sat. The desk could be seen from the front window, but Doyle moved the chair back into the darkness. It was getting darker now that the sun had slipped below the horizon. Doyle waited, after turning on one small desk lamp.

He had done surveillance a number of times and could stay awake for hours. So he wasn't worried about falling asleep and missing his chance to catch the killer. He sat there watching the door, then thought about setting something in front of the door to make noise in case he did doze off. It could happen. He took a chair and set it in behind the door.

Doyle's Paradise

If someone could open the lock, they would have to move the chair and Doyle would hear it.

Doyle looked around the room and realized that there were three windows that an intruder could come through. Now he was concerned. He would have to be extra alert.

Two hours later he heard movement on the porch. He drew his Sig 9 and went to the door waiting. He heard the knob twist and so he quietly moved the chair, grabbed the inside door handle and pulled it open. He held out his weapon and found it was Morris.

"What are you doing here, Albert?" Doyle demanded, still aiming his gun at Morris's face.

"Don't shoot! I'm innocent," Morris said as Doyle pulled him into the building, closing the door.

"Talk quickly, Albert. Why are you here at almost midnight trying to get in this bungalow?"

Doyle sat Morris down and leaned into him, with his weapon still on Morris' nose.

"Doyle, you have to believe me. I had nothing to do with Kabe's death. The only reason I'm here right now is because I have a master door lock card and because of the note I got." The man was sweating rain, and looking scared.

"What note?" Doyle asked.

Morris pulled a piece of paper from his shirt pocket and handed it to Doyle. Doyle moved away from Morris, but kept his gun on him. He opened the paper with one hand and read the typed note.

"Morris, you will do what I say, or die! There should be a briefcase in the bungalow of the late Mr. Kabe. You will get it for me and place it on the large flat rock at Breaker's Point and leave. I mean business. I killed Kabe and you will be next if you don't cooperate. Do it tonight!"

"How did you get this?"

"It was on my desk earlier. I didn't question it, I wanted to live."

"Where is Breaker's Point?" Doyle asked.

"It's around the other side of the island, beyond the sink holes, so we never go there."

"Well, you'll go there tonight," Doyle said and went to get the briefcase. He handed it to Morris and stood back. "Take it and leave quietly. Put it on that rock and run away fast, keeping your head down."

"Are you going to protect me?" Morris asked.

Doyle's Paradise

"I'll see what I can do. Just do what the note said. Hopefully, whoever wrote it, didn't see you enter here and see me. Go take it out and drop it off."

Doyle went behind the door and opened it for Morris. "Be careful and watch out for trouble. Are you walking there?"

Morris said he was.

"I'll try and be close by. Don't be a hero, just drop it and run."

Doyle waited a couple minutes before he left the building. He figured whoever left the note was waiting by the rock to get the briefcase. Doyle figured the mystery man would destroy the case rather than try and bring it back to New York. He could hear Morris tramping through the brush and tried to keep as close as possible without giving himself away.

About a half hour later, Doyle passed a few signs warning not to proceed this way. He hoped if he stayed on the path that Morris was taking, he wouldn't fall into a sink hole. They continued on until he heard Morris stop. The moon was half full and gave a little light to the night and the rocks. He could see from his hiding place in the ferns and brush, that Morris put the case on a large flat stone in a clearing.

Morris did what Doyle told him to do. He dropped the case and ran like hell. Morris went right by Doyle without seeing him, which pleased him. Doyle turned his attention to the case on the rock and waited. He could see the case very clearly in the moonlight and figured he would have a good shot with his gun when someone came to get the case. He waited, watching around the area. There wasn't much cover to hide him if he left the path going to the rocks where it was all stone and the water lapping the shore.

If this person had no idea that Morris was followed, then he or she should have taken the bait already. This worried Doyle. Would this turn out to be a bust, needlessly jeopardizing Morris' life by allowing someone to follow him? Or could the killer be cautious also? He'd wait it out.

This became a cat and mouse game. Each waiting for the other to move and take the bait. Doyle knew he could hold out for a long time, he'd done it before. If the killer didn't take the case, he wondered if he should retrieve it or leave it there. Would he have to wait all night?

Doyle was waiting patiently for movement, when he got his wish. He could see a pair of hands coming up from the other side of the flat rock. No body, just hands and arms slowly moving towards the case. Doyle had no shot, nothing to hit but arms and hands. Too small a target. He knew he had to break out and approach the rock where the person was. He figured he could traverse the distance and stop the unseen person before he could get away, so he made his move.

He ran towards the figure and when he got there the arms, hands and intruder were gone. Doyle stood looking dumbfounded. There was no way the person could have eluded Doyle.

*

Chapter 13

Doyle looked around the area and saw no one. He turned to the briefcase and was amazed that it was also gone. The killer had made off with it. Maybe the killer didn't know Doyle had tried to jump him. He must have grabbed the briefcase and disappeared with it. But how?

Doyle took out his key ring and turned on the tiny flashlight that was attached to the ring. He shined the light around the flat rock and saw it looked like a table on two smaller rocks below it, then he saw it. A small sinkhole under the rock table. He tried to shine the light down the hole but it veered off down a tunnel going to who knows where.

Doyle thought about going after the suspect, but even he wasn't crazy enough to drop down into a sinkhole and go off getting lost underground. He'd talk to Morris, since he seemed to know the island and find out how these holes and tunnels were connected.

"Well, so much for my big bust," Doyle said to himself quietly. He turned to go back on the path he came through and followed it back to the bungalows. A light was on in Marge's building, but Doyle figured on leaving them alone.

"What are you doing standing there in the dark, mister?" came a voice from the side of Marge's bungalow. Doyle spun with his gun in hand, waiting for whoever spoke to either come out or shoot. "Whoa, dear, don't shoot the woman you share your bed with," Poppy said as she came forward from the darkness.

"What the hell are you doing skulking around outside?" Doyle asked as she came to him.

"I was just getting some air and getting away from Marge and Lorna. Those two can really talk up a storm." Poppy put her arms around Doyle and asked, "Did your suspect show up?"

Doyle laughed slightly and said, "I have a story to tell you. Let's sit on the porch and talk."

Doyle's Paradise

They went to their bungalow and sat on the porch. Doyle related everything that happened after he went into Lorna's bungalow. He covered the strange incident at the flat rock and how the suspect escaped through a hole in the ground.

"Maybe he's a mole person," Poppy said with a grin. "Maybe the mad scientist changed him."

"You're not helping," he said. "I have to find out where all these holes and tunnels go to. It's late and too dark to chase the criminal tonight. I'll go see Morris in the morning. I need a couple hours sleep to recharge."

"If the killer came through the holes, he would have to know the island. I don't think any of the guests would be that familiar with the island. Maybe it's one of the staff?"

"Or Dante, I didn't trust him from the start," Doyle said with a grin.

"No, he's the mastermind and he has his staff do his bidding. Murder, intrigue and espionage."

"You should write this down and make a book out of it. Now I'm going to bed. You may as well hang in with Marge and Lorna. They may need you. I don't know if the killer knows what to look for in the briefcase and since I took out all the really damaging papers, he may come looking for them."

"Will do, chief. I'll protect the innocent women," Poppy mugged her words.

"You're a little loopy tonight, have you been drinking? Let me smell your breath."

Poppy blew at him and laughed. She stood and wiggled her butt, then went across the way to Marge's bungalow. Doyle just sat there in amazement at his goofy girlfriend.

He sat for a couple minutes and then decided to get some sleep. He stood just as he heard someone coming through the brush. He pulled his gun and waited. More thrashing around and then out came Morris.

"Albert, did you lose your way?"

"No, Mr. Doyle. I had to see if you were all right. I ran until I came out in the compound. I thought about you being back there with the killer and started to worry."

"Well, thank you for that, Albert. May I call you Al, Albert is so formal?"

"Sure, most people on the staff call me Butch. I don't know how that started but I didn't argue."

Doyle's Paradise

"Okay, but I'll call you Al. I'm glad you're here. I was going to see you in the morning, but since you're here, I need to talk to you."

"Whatever, glad to help."

"Let's talk inside," Doyle said and took Morris into his bungalow. "Have a chair and we can talk."

They sat and Morris waited for Doyle to speak. He told the young man what had happened after Morris left the briefcase and ran off.

"That side of the island is full of holes and tunnels. Mostly from volcanic actions that created this island. I've explored the tunnels a couple times myself. It's like a honeycomb down there."

"From under the flat rock at Breaker's Point, where does that tunnel lead to?" Doyle asked.

"They all interconnect and go everywhere. A person would have to know where they were going or they could be lost down there for a long time. Some of the tunnels are so narrow, that a person could barely squeeze through."

"You've been down there, how did you manage to find your way out?"

"I took a can of white spray paint and marked the way I came. I would just backtrack when I got confused."

"So if the killer came up through the hole under the flat rock, took the briefcase and went back down, where would he go?"

"Well, most of those tunnels have a sinkhole that a person could get out of. He might have grabbed the case and gone over to escape out a sinkhole nearby."

Doyle thought about that. He hadn't heard any movement in the jungle after the suspect took the case. Maybe he was waiting for Doyle to leave. "Whatever, I'm going to get some sleep. I'll talk more to you in the morning."

Doyle stood and took Morris to the door. "Thanks for the concern, Albert. We'll talk later."

Morris nodded and left. Doyle locked the door, he didn't figure Poppy would slip in and he had the door lock card. He went to the bed, dropping his clothes and flopped down.

He could hear a pounding on his door and mumbled, "Now, what?" He sat up and looked at his watch, it was seven in the morning. He slept most the night. "Sleep should feel longer than that, damn it."

He went to the door and yelled, "Who is it?"

Doyle's Paradise

"Room service," came the reply.

"Just leave it at the door, I'll get it later." He stood laughing as Poppy banged on the door.

He unlocked the door and let her in. "How are the hostages doing this morning?"

"Lorna is moaning about her husband and Marge is knitting. I had to get away from them. Did you sleep all right?"

"I did, and I had dreams about you and me running naked on the beach. By the way, I haven't seen where this nude beach is."

"Never mind. You have a killer to find before you go and ogle naked women."

There was quick knocking at the door. Doyle mumbled an obscenity and went to open it. He found one of Morris' security men standing, looking upset. "Mr. Doyle, can you come quickly? Morris was shot."

*

Chapter 14

Doyle didn't usually feel a shudder when shocked, but this news sent a shudder up his spine. He turned to Poppy, "Let's go." They left the bungalow and followed the young man, moving quickly.

"What happened?" Doyle asked him.

"They found him near his sleeping quarters on the ground. The doctor has him in his clinic, but doesn't think he can help him. I understand that he was hit in the head."

Doyle felt another shudder as they approached the clinic. The young man opened the door for Doyle and Poppy as they moved past him. Dante was standing just outside the examination room looking in. "Mr. Doyle, this is getting worse. Do you have any leads as to who this killer is?"

"I wish I could say I did, but this turn of events is something I was afraid might happen. I'll explain." Doyle told Dante about the late night adventure with the briefcase and meeting Morris later. He showed Dante the note Morris had on him. "I think Morris must have been coming back to his quarters and was shot because I followed him. This does not make me happy."

The doctor came out of the exam room and said, "He has a bullet lodged in his head, somewhere. I don't have the equipment or the expertise to help him. I think he may be bleeding inside his skull. I may be able to drain off the blood, but he'll need a surgical procedure to save him from further system damage and to remove the bullet." He looked at Doyle and said, "This is that time I said would be bad that we have no communication to the mainland."

"Yes, we do. Hold on." Doyle turned and ran out the door. He was gone for about five minutes when he came back in. He had the satellite phone.

"Mr. Doyle, how long have you had that?" Dante asked.

"Since yesterday, I'll explain later. First we need to call for a medevac chopper. Doc, do you know how to reach one on the main island?"

"I do. Does that thing work?"

"I don't know, I haven't tried it yet." Doyle flipped the power switch and it lit up. He held it to his ear and could hear a sound. He handed it to the doctor who went to his desk and pulled out a book of numbers. He was hitting the keypad and listened. He gave a thumbs up as someone answered from the hospital he called. He quickly explained what had happened and requested a chopper to evacuate the patient. They talked briefly then the doctor hung up.

"You'll need to get some of the security to clear an area for the chopper to land," the doctor told Dante. He went out to take care of it.

"Where did you get this phone?" The doctor asked Doyle, handing it back to him.

"Kabe brought it with him. I found it in his belongings last night. I'm glad it came in handy. What can you do for Morris now?"

"Just try to keep him alive, until they get here. They'll have medical staff on the chopper that can start to work on him until they get to the hospital."

"Doc, I know you're a general practitioner, not having the knowledge to speculate on his chances. What do you think?"

"Slim to none. I wish I could say more but his blood pressure is dropping and he's unresponsive to stimuli. His only hope is the chopper and the hospital."

"I think Dante should take a hard look at the need for communications with civilization," Doyle said.

Doyle's Paradise

Poppy said she was going outside to watch for the helicopter. Doyle went in the exam room and stayed with Morris.

The helicopter moved much faster than the island plane so it only took twenty minutes for it to arrive. The security men had cleared an area and put down a bed sheet on the ground. Someone took spray paint and labeled the sheet with a big 'H' in orange.

The chopper landed safely and medical staff streamed out following Dante to the clinic. They strapped Morris to a stretcher and took him to the chopper. They had an intravenous tube attached to him and were checking his vital signs. Dante said he was going with the chopper and said that the doctor was now in charge. They all climbed on the big whirlybird, which lifted off and shot across the sky back to the main island.

"Damn, I shouldn't have let him go back to his quarters alone. This is my fault. I want this bastard really bad now."

Poppy put her hand on his shoulder. "You can't blame yourself. Even if you had walked him back, he may still have been shot and you along with him."

That didn't help Doyle's mood. He turned to the four security officers and said, "Gather everyone in the meeting hall now." Most of the guests were milling around watching the helicopter, so it was easy to get them together.

Doyle was mad now, he didn't like being the reason some innocent person was harmed. He waited until everyone was in the building and stood by the stage with the doctor. One of the security men came up and said they had everyone including the staff. Doyle saw Lorna and Marge standing at the back of the room and smiled at them.

"Everyone on the island is here now, no stragglers?" he asked the man.

"Everyone that we have registered. I had them check the roster."

"Good, have your men watch the doors to be sure no one leaves." Doyle turned to the doc and said, "Shall we get everyone up to date?"

"Mr. Doyle, Dante said as he was leaving that I was in charge. I'm not a leader by any means. I'm a doctor and happy with it. I'm turning over the position to you. You're in charge now."

"Thanks Doc. I won't disappoint you," Doyle said with a smile. He went up on the stage and said, "Let's have your undivided attention up here. I have a number of things to cover. First, the young man who was in charge of security was shot this morning. You all saw the helicopter take him away. We're hoping they can do something for him. Now, he shouldn't have been shot. There is someone on this island who has murdered one man and attempted murder on another. I'm not happy about this and I will tear this island up to find that person. This room presently contains all the people who are on this island. That means one of you is a cold-blooded killer."

He stepped off the stage and went to the edge of the group of guests. Everyone was silent, not one sound was heard.

"I don't like cold-blooded killers, I detest them. I think cold-blooded killers should be quickly executed and their body dropped in the ocean for the sharks to feed on. I want everyone to look at the people around you. One of them is a killer. Do you think it's someone you know? Is this person real good at pretending he, or she, is here to enjoy their vacation?"

He moved around the crowd looking at each person he walked by, watching for a sign. "I'm sorry you came here for a chance at paradise, only to have it turn into hell. The faster I find this person, the faster you can relax and enjoy your stay. I want this person. It's my personal vendetta to find him, or her. You won't get away from me. I'll find you. When I do, you'll regret me being here. Trust me when I say that."

Doyle pulled out his Sig and fired twice into the ceiling. Everyone jumped and some screamed. He watched them to see who wasn't bothered by the shots. Two men didn't flinch. He made note of them.

"As I say, I'm not playing. I came here with my girlfriend and we brought my business secretary to relax and enjoy ourselves. Now my vacation is ruined. As I said, I'm not happy." He stood letting that sink in.

"Now, Mr. Dante left with the chopper to go to the hospital with Morris. As he left, he put the doctor in charge of the island. Doctor Hakon has decided he doesn't want the responsibility, so he gave it to me. If you have any problems or concerns about what's happening, let me know. I will be watching, so be careful what you do." He paused again, then said, "Okay, go out and enjoy yourselves."

*

Chapter 15

He smiled, turned to the doctor and asked, "So, do you think I stirred them up?"

"Firing your gun into the ceiling was a nice touch. It frightened the crap out of me," Doc Hakon said with a laugh.

Doyle's Paradise

"Can you show me exactly where Albert was found?" Doyle asked, as Poppy came over to him.

"Sure, follow me." They left the building with Marge and Lorna now following. The doctor took them to where they found Morris on the ground. Doyle looked back to see the four security men were coming towards them.

"This is the spot, you can still see some blood," the doctor said. "It was a clean shot, luckily he didn't bleed out."

Doyle was scanning the area to see where a person would hide to fire on the victim. It was mostly dense jungle, but there were a number of small buildings that were the living quarters for the island staff.

"If I were a sniper, where would my best advantage be?" Doyle said, mostly to himself.

"That clump of bushes over there," Poppy offered. "Or the side of that building with the vines growing up."

Doyle looked at both places and agreed. He went to the first clump of bushes and examined around the grounds.

"Think you might find shell casings?" Poppy asked.

100

"Depends on what type of weapon it was. A hand gun doesn't eject shells, but most rifles will." He kicked around the ground and found a couple of cigarette butts.

"Do you allow the staff to smoke?" Doyle asked the doctor.

"No, it's one of Dante's pet peeves. No smoking allowed. He can't really stop the guests, but there are signs in the bungalows about not smoking in the buildings."

Doyle bent down and picked up the two butts, reading the name on the tips. "Marlboros. More of a man's cigarette."

"That's discriminatory," Poppy said. "I know women who smoke them."

"And I'll bet they're tough women," Doyle said with a grin.

"Okay, they are," Poppy agreed.

"These are fairly fresh. The weather hasn't gotten to them. I'd say our killer may have left them here."

"This spot is fairly close to where Morris fell. Wouldn't you say the shot came from a handgun? A rifle from here would be overkill," Poppy observed.

101

"I'll agree with that, but again, no sound of gunfire. He must have silenced the weapon. The killer may even have been close to Kabe when he was shot, since the wife was hanging back," Doyle said.

"Whatever gun the killer used, the point is he murdered one man and attempted to kill another," the doctor said.

"And we need to find him. Let's go see who smokes cigarettes, first," Doyle said and turned to the security men. "Okay, guys, I want you to spread out and check on the guests, watching to see if they smoke. Then carefully retrieve a butt if they drop it or throw it out. See if it's a Marlboro, if not, keep checking."

The men agreed and went off. "Since no one questions security moving around the island, they can do the job much easier," Doyle continued. "I'm thinking of letting these men carry the rifles that are locked up. Do you know if they are trained in using rifles?" he asked the doctor.

"I know that Dante wanted them to have training in the proper use of the rifles, so I assume they were trained."

"It's something to think about. We may also need to search bungalows to see if the killer was dumb enough to keep his weapon close by. Since he shot Morris, we know he hasn't disposed of the weapon, yet."

"I'm sure all the guests think you're crazy at this point, so I'm sure the killer will be extra careful now," the doc said.

"I'm still puzzled why he would trap himself on this island after shooting two people. Killing Kabe would have been much easier back in New York," Doyle wondered. "I'd like to look at the books with the reservations. Shall we go to the office?"

They left the staff quarters and went around to the office. The busty girl was behind the desk when they came in. Poppy poked Doyle in the back. He grinned back at her.

"Tamra, Mr. Doyle wants to see the reservation logs," the doc asked of the girl. She pulled out a large ledger type book and set it on the counter.

"Just how do you know who is coming to the island, since you can't communicate with the airport where we came through?" Doyle asked.

"My sister, at the airport entry point, gets the reservations and signs everyone in. They all wait to board the plane and she gives the sheet with the information to the pilot. He passes it to me and I log everyone here in this book."

Doyle's Paradise

"Do you have the sheet of info from this group?"

She opened the book to the back and pulled out a sheet of paper and handed it to Doyle. "This is the master list of when everyone placed their reservations and signed in," she said.

Doyle opened the folded sheet and set it on the counter. Poppy looked over his shoulder at the paper.

"I can see here when each person contacted your company to make arrangements to come to the island. The Kabes placed their reservations a week ago. Only two other couples signed up after them. Everyone else filed over a month before." Doyle took a pad of paper from the counter and wrote the names of the late-comers.

"You think maybe these people came to the island because the Kabes were coming here?" Poppy asked.

"Makes sense. The others couldn't have known the Kabes were coming here. I'd say they were followed."

Doyle turned to Marge and Lorna, "Aren't you two getting bored following us around?"

"Oh, heavens no, Arthur," Marge said happily. "I've never seen you investigating since I've worked for you. This is exciting."

"It's a lot of leg work. So hang in there and if you feel like going off, go ahead."

"I will," Marge said.

"Doc, I think you should contact the hospital and see how Albert is doing," Doyle said handing the satellite phone to him.

"I was thinking the same," he replied and took the phone. He went to the side of the room and dialed.

Doyle looked at Poppy and said, "I'm making up a story in my head."

"Am I in it?" Poppy asked with a sly smile.

"No, this takes place in New York. Kabe takes damaging papers and his own reports on the illegal activities of the company. Then he wants to get out of the country so he can work on his case against them. What better place than a secluded island in the Pacific, thousands of miles from New York? But somehow his bosses find out and they send someone to kill him and retrieve the files. That could explain why the hit man is on this island. To stop Kabe before he contacts the authorities."

Doyle's Paradise

"Wow, you thought that up all by yourself?" Poppy mugged.

Doyle stared at her, then said, "Why do I even tell you anything?"

"Because I'm good in bed," she said quietly.

"Okay, good point. Now the killer could have waited until just before they were scheduled to leave the island, but if he knew Kabe could contact the authorities, he had to act fast and stop Kabe. Then to prevent being exposed, he sends Albert to retrieve the briefcase. But how did he know about the tunnels at the flat rock?"

"So, you haven't thought this all the way through?"

"If I had, I'd know who the killer was, smart ass," Doyle said.

*

Chapter 16

Doyle turned to Lorna. "I need to ask you, when did your husband decide that he wanted to come here? Was it his idea?"

She paused, then said, "Yes, it was his idea. He surprised me on short notice that we were coming here. I wasn't going to argue, it sounded so good for our honeymoon."

"Did you tell anyone else where you were going?"

"That was the funny thing, he said not to tell anyone. He had his reasons and said he'd explain later."

"Now, Lorna, I have to ask and please be truthful. Did you tell anyone about your trip and where you were going? It's important."

She paused, thinking. "I was having a hard time keeping it to myself, but yes, I did. Elmer's secretary at work called and said she needed to know where we were going in case they had to contact him for business concerns. I figured it would be important that they knew and told her." Lorna stopped and realized what she did. "Oh, no. I told them where to

107

find Elmer. I gave him away." She started to tear up so Marge took her to the couch in the lobby.

Doyle went to her. "We don't know if that's the reason. So don't blame yourself. There's lots of ways they could have followed him."

"You said his company wanted him dead. I told them where he was going. I let him down." She broke down into more tears.

"Marge, take her back to your bungalow and let her rest." Doyle helped them up. "Lorna, we will find out what happened, so don't think this was your fault."

The two women left the building. "I hate to say it, but she probably did give her husband away to the company. I'd like to prove it wasn't her slip that did it."

"When we find the killer, you can torture him to find out. You'd enjoy that."

"Yes, I would," Doyle said as the doctor came back.

"Well, some good news. Morris went through the operation fine. They removed the bullet and have him in an induced coma. Which is good in his case. He's alive and may survive without any problems."

"May survive? That doesn't sound promising," Doyle said.

"They won't know until he stabilizes. It's the best they can hope for now. They also said we got him to the hospital in time," the doctor said and handed the phone back to Doyle.

Doyle stood staring at the phone. "I may call Oscar in New York and have him look into the company. Maybe I need to call my FBI friend Kent Simmons and explain the situation to him. I'm sure the government would love the information I have."

"Where did you put the information? If the killer can't find it in the briefcase he may figure you have it," Poppy said.

"Let's go back and go through the papers and see what goodies we can find. Just to give Kent something to chew on. And I hope the killer comes knocking at our door." Doyle said. "Then we need to check on these people on the late list."

Doyle thanked the doctor as he said he was going back to his clinic. Doyle led Poppy back to their bungalow and went in. He went to the corner of the room, over to the small dresser on the floor and lifted it one end. He reached under and pulled out a plastic bag. He took the bag to the desk and pulled out the papers inside.

Doyle's Paradise

"That wasn't the best hiding place," Poppy said. "I could have found that in no time."

"Then, next time you hide it."

Poppy was standing next to the door when there came a knocking. She pulled her .38 and went to the door. "Mr. Doyle, I'm David, one of the security officers," came a voice through the door. Poppy held out her gun and opened it. The young man standing there was shocked to see a gun pointed at him. "Hey, I'm one of the good guys," he sputtered.

Poppy put her gun back and invited the man in. "What do you have, David?" Doyle asked.

"Well, sir, we followed everyone like you said. Out of all those people we found, twelve were smokers. Out of the twelve, three smoked Marlboros. I have their names," he beamed proudly.

Doyle went to him and took the paper he held out. "Very good, David. Morris would be proud. And, so you can tell the men, Morris is out of surgery and he's stable so far."

"Thank you, sir," David said and turned to go out, giving Poppy a wary eye. He left.

"I think I frightened him," Poppy said.

"You have that effect on men. You frightened me the first time I met you."

"Ah, yes, the ice queen was what you called me."

"No, Oscar called you that, I just agreed."

Doyle was studying the list of smokers. He pulled his list of guests who placed late reservations after the Kabes. "I see only one guest that came late on the island and they smoke Marlboros. Larry Janin and his wife, Janice. Interesting, according to David's list, she's the one who smokes the cigarettes."

"I told you women smoke them. Shall we go interrogate the Janins?" Poppy said.

"Do you want to hide the papers this time?"

"You go outside and I'll hide them. Then when we come back, you see if you can find them," Poppy smirked.

Doyle smiled and went outside. After a couple minutes, Poppy came out. "All done," she grinned.

"If I find them, what do I get?" Doyle asked.

"Anything you want in bed tonight."

Doyle's Paradise

"Now that's an incentive. Prepare for your doom." They went back to the compound and found the security officers standing, talking.

One of them came to Doyle and said. "You tell us what you need and we'll follow you."

"Thank you. I'll need you guys to help bring two guests to the office. Help me locate the Larry Janin couple."

The young man ran off and went into the office. About two minutes later he came out with a slip of paper and handed it to Doyle. "They're in bungalow five."

Doyle signaled to the other men to follow and said, "Lead the way."

On the way down the path to the Janin bungalow, one man asked, "Is Albert going to be all right? We talked and would be willing to give blood if it helps."

Doyle smiled and said, "I'll let you know, but thanks for the offer."

They arrived at the bungalow and Doyle banged on the door. There was no answer. Doyle asked David if they carried master door lock keys. David said they did and took his out, handing it to Doyle.

Poppy took out her gun, as did Doyle, and told the men to stand back. They did. He took the key card and put it in the door lock. It clicked and he pushed the door open.

"Janin, it's Doyle. If you are in there, come out quietly." There was no response. He looked to Poppy and told her to be careful. He went in low, as Poppy came in high. The bungalow was empty.

They stood in the middle of the room as Doyle went to the bathroom, carefully pushing open the door.

"Okay, we have a problem," Doyle said. Poppy came over and looked in. There was a pool of blood and in the middle was a woman, dead on the floor.

*

Chapter 17

"Okay, now we arm all the men." He turned to David and said, "Go back to the security office and take the rifles. Then load them and fill your pockets with ammo. Be on the watch for Larry Janin. He's now our suspect in the murder of Kabe, shooting of Morris and now of his wife. Also send the doctor here to take care of the body. Come back with him to help."

The men left the building as Doyle looked around the room. The luggage was on the bed and opened. He sorted through it to find anything that would help. There was nothing but clothes and personal hygiene things. Poppy found a purse and dumped the contents on the desk. She sorted through the contents and found a wallet.

"Doyle, take a look at this," Poppy said holding the wallet out for him. He took it and read what she was taking about.

"This woman is not his wife, or she didn't change her name. Her name was Janice Wall, and the address is in New York. That wasn't on the reservation list. It said they came from Arizona. Lies and deceit. This has to be our killer."

"The wife or the husband?" Poppy asked.

"You just aren't happy with a simple explanation."

"Never. And you shouldn't be either," she said.

"I never take the easy way out. Now we have to find Janin."

"Maybe he's hiding in the sinkholes and tunnels."

"Oh, man, I hope not. I'm not going down there," Doyle groaned.

"You have claustrophobia, don't you?" she asked

"Don't tell anyone. I think we need to smoke him out if he's down there."

They were talking when they heard someone on the porch. They both pulled their guns as the door opened. A man came in, then looked shocked when he saw Doyle and Poppy.

"What are you doing in here, Mr. Doyle?" he asked.

"Are you Larry Janin?" he asked still holding his gun on the man.

"I am, what is this about?"

Doyle's Paradise

Doyle stepped aside to reveal the body on the bathroom floor. The man looked down and cried out, "Oh my God, Janice. What did you do to her?" He headed to the room, but Doyle stopped him and held him back.

"Stop, Janin. She's dead. We found her like this. Talk to me, where have you been?"

"I...I went to the office to see if we could leave the island. They said we couldn't until the plane came in four days. What happened to her?"

"Sit down and talk to us." He pushed the man to the bed and sat him down. "Where are you from?"

He looked at Doyle and said, "Arizona."

"Let me see your driver's license." Doyle asked.

Janin took it out and handed the card to Doyle. He examined it and handed it back.

Doyle said, "Her driver's license says she was from New York."

"She was. We weren't married. I was having an affair with her. We worked for the same company but in different states. We met through company work conferences."

"What company?"

"New York Heavy Equipment and Sales," he said.

Doyle looked at Poppy. "It's the company Kabe worked for," he said as he turned to Janin and asked, "Did you know Elmer Kabe?"

Janin looked confused. "I have no idea who he is."

"Your girlfriend was working at the same company as Kabe in New York, she must have known him. Are you sure she didn't mention it?"

"No. Was the man who was murdered working for New York Heavy Equipment and Sales?"

"He was. As an attorney. Who murdered your girlfriend?"

"How the hell would I know? I left her here an hour ago. There are people in the main office who can verify that. I just now came back to find you in my bungalow. Maybe you murdered her."

Doyle pulled the man up by his shirt and said into his face, "I want the killer that's doing this. If you are lying to me, I'll drop you into one of the sinkholes after I put a bullet into your head. Now don't give me your smart ass comments."

He pushed the man back down and asked, "You came here at the last minute, on reservations made about a week before you arrived, why?"

"It was Janice's idea. She wanted to get away from her husband and come here to paradise, she said."

"Did you know about this island before your girlfriend mentioned it?"

"I never heard about it."

Doyle looked at Poppy and took her aside, "I'm wondering if this woman was the hit man. But who killed her? This is getting complicated."

"You'll be able to figure it out, I'm sure."

"Thanks for your confidence. Now what do you think about his statements?"

"I'm not seeing any lies, but I could be wrong."

"Same here," he said as the door opened and in came David with the doctor.

"Aren't you getting tired of dead bodies?" the doctor asked.

"Yes, I am," Doyle said with a grin. "What can you tell me about this woman?"

"Let me look." He went to the bathroom and leaned down to the body. He took a few minutes to examine her, then said, "Looks like it was a .22 again. The bullet penetrated her head up through the throat. I did some checking in our library and there is a subsonic round that makes little noise. The Aquila 550 fps powderless .22 LR rounds. They work off the primer alone. The only noise this gun makes with these rounds is the click of the hammer, then the thump when the bullet strikes the target. They aren't real powerful, but at close range they will kill. I'd say the killer used these rounds. Just my opinion as to why no loud noises."

"Sounds like something a hit man would know about," Doyle said as he stood back from the bathroom. He turned to Janin and said, "I'm not letting you off this easily. Now how did she know about this island?"

"She said her boss mentioned it and it sounded like a good place to get away."

"Why the short notice? She placed the reservations about a week ago."

"She said she had vacation time coming and wanted to get away. I had some time coming and took it. She arranged the reservations and we went to

119

the airport where we caught the plane to come to this island. What's going on? Why was she murdered?"

"I'll tell you when we figure it out. Now I have to call an associate who's in New York and have him do some checking on your company. There has to be a link between your girlfriend and Kabe. Don't leave town," Doyle said half-jokingly.

He went back to Doc Hakon as the security officers were putting the woman on a stretcher. "Another side of beef for the meat locker?" Doyle joked.

"Yeah, you could say that. I may need your phone to call for someone to pick up these bodies. That would involve the police."

"They have no jurisdiction on this island unless invited. Let's leave this to ourselves until we find the killer. Keep them on ice for now."

"You're the boss. I'll wrap her and introduce her to the late Mr. Kabe," the doc said.

Doyle frowned and said, "I have a feeling she already knew Kabe. I have to check on that."

*

Chapter 18

The doctor, with the security men, took the woman's body out as Janin followed them. They went down the path as Doyle and Poppy came out of the bungalow. They sat on the steps of the porch.

Doyle had the paper with the names of late guests on it and read it one more time. He took his pen and wrote the real name of the dead woman.

"I'll call Oscar and have him go nose around the company and see what he can find out," Doyle said. He took the phone out and dialed. After a few minutes of connecting through the satellites, Oscar answered his phone. Doyle put it on speaker.

"Oscar, it's Doyle, can you hear me?"

"Why wouldn't I hear you? Is your phone messed up? Hey, I thought you couldn't use phones in paradise?"

"I'm calling you on a satellite phone, which I'll explain in a minute. Poppy's here listening. First I have a tale to tell you, so listen carefully."

Doyle's Paradise

He covered everything from when they found the woman hovering over her dead husband's body. He told of the other shootings and the dead woman they just found.

"I thought you two were going for some rest and relaxation. You should write a book. What do you want me to do?"

"I need you to look up New York Heavy Equipment and Sales and do some snooping. Whatever you can find out. If you have to talk to my friend Kent Simmons in the FBI, I'm sure he will help. I'll call him and explain, then give him your number."

"Who am I looking for?"

"Well, they're both here and very dead, but find out what they did at the company. Mostly the woman, we know the man was a lawyer and he had the dirty dealings on the company. We think he was murdered for the papers. I have them safely put away and will give them to the proper authorities when we get back to civilization." Doyle read the names of the woman and Kabe. Oscar said he'd see what he could find and be expecting a call from Simmons.

"Good, write down my number, so you can call me back." He gave Oscar the number and they finished the call. He looked at Poppy, "Now to get the FBI in on this."

He dialed the number he had for his friend and waited. When Simmons answered, Doyle started the speaker again.

"Art, good to hear from you. What's up? I don't hear from you, so it must be a crime in progress."

"It is and you're going to love this mess." Doyle told Kent about their adventures of the last three days as he listened.

"Man, you don't just have a simple murder, do you? Company espionage and collusion, dirty dealings and murder. Why am I not surprised? What do you need from me?"

"Call Oscar in New York and see if he needs help snooping around the company. You can open doors better than he can."

"Actually I need a trip to the East coast. I may just jump on our jet and visit him. Shoot me the number."

Doyle read Oscar's number and said, "If what my lawyer explained is true, this company is cooking the books for tax evasion. Maybe you have some connections with the Treasury Department?"

"I do and will be more than happy to call. Thanks for the heads up on this. Since you have no communications on the island, if you can fax me the papers when you get back to Hawaii, I'll pass them along."

"Will do. Now, I have a killer to catch on the island, call me when you have something."

They finished up and Doyle said to Poppy, "I want to talk to Lorna and see what she knows about Janice Wall."

They stood and walked around to their bungalow. Marge was on her porch knitting and waved to them. They went to her as Doyle asked, "Where's Lorna?"

"She said she wanted to go down to the beach to relax. I didn't think it would hurt."

"Okay, thanks." They turned down the path to the beach and found Lorna sitting on the grass above the sand. She looked back and smiled.

"Any luck with finding the killer?" she asked.

"Lorna, I need to ask you some questions. Feel like talking?"

She agreed and Doyle sat next to her. Poppy sat on the other side.

"Lorna, did you know a woman named Janice Wall?"

"I did. She was Elmer's secretary. She was the one who called me about where we were going. Why?"

Doyle was surprised by this revelation. "Did you know she was on the island?"

Lorna stiffened and said, "No, where is she?"

"Right now getting wrapped up to join your husband. She was murdered a little less than an hour ago."

"Oh, my God. Is this madness going to stop? Why is the company murdering people who work for them?"

"We have an idea why your husband was murdered but the Wall woman is a puzzle. I was hoping you might know. Was she friendly with your husband?"

"If you're asking if my husband and Wall ever hooked up, no. I never got any idea that they were messing around."

"Well, she was on the island with a man who says he and she were having an affair. Wall has a husband back in New York."

125

Doyle's Paradise

Lorna looked at Doyle with a strange expression. "I was under the impression that she was single. I had joked with Elmer about staying away from her."

"Single? The man she was with said she had a husband." Doyle looked over to Poppy and she had a concerned look. "Why would Janin lie?"

"Janin?" Lorna said. "Is that Larry Janin?"

"You know him?" Doyle asked.

"Never met him, but Elmer mentioned his name once when he came back from a company conference. Janin was an employee in Arizona and was talking about coming to New York. Elmer got to know him and said he wasn't a very nice guy to know."

"That's interesting. Janin said he didn't know your husband when I mentioned his name. I think we need to talk to Janin again." Doyle got up, followed by Poppy. "Let's get to the clinic fast. Janin went with the body."

They went back up the path and followed it to the compound going to the clinic. They went in and found Doc and two security men wrapping the body.

"Walter, where's Janin?" Doyle asked the doc.

"Haven't seen him since he followed us to the edge of the compound, and then went off somewhere."

Doyle turned and took Poppy to the waiting room. "He's hiding, I just feel it. Okay, let's try this on. The company wants Kabe dead and his papers destroyed. Wall finds out Kabe is leaving and calls Lorna to find out where they were going. The company brought in a hit man, who turns out to be Janin. They had him working in the company, probably on retainer for killing people. Janin needs to get on the island but it would look suspicious if he came alone, so he brings Wall. He kills Kabe then tries to get the briefcase through Morris. That goes wrong and he attempts to kill Morris, but doesn't succeed. Something happened between Janin and Wall that caused him to shoot her. How am I doing so far?"

"Good, now is Janin hiding somewhere in your theory?"

Doyle was looking around the island. It was jungle and mountains. Not big mountains but ones formed by volcanic activity. "There could be any number of places to hide. But how is he going to get off the island? He can't take the plane by force. With you and me having guns, then the four security men with rifles, it would be a futile attempt."

"Don't forget Marge with her cannon," Poppy smiled.

"Ah, yes, she's the most dangerous."

*

Chapter 19

"Where shall we start?" Poppy asked as they walked out of the clinic.

Doyle was watching the guests having a good time, despite the crimes committed around them. There were couples playing tennis, some whacking a croquet mallet or playing cards at the tables. But everyone was having a good time.

"People are resilient. They adapt and accept their lives. Well, most people. The evil ones want more than they have. Money, gold, jewels, power, whatever. And they will kill to get it or protect what they have. Kabe was shaking the tree when it came to the company's corruption. So they eliminated him and those that came along behind him. I hope Oscar and Kent find something to shake up the company."

He smiled at his girlfriend and said, "Let's go catch a killer."

"Lead the way," she replied.

"If only I knew where to lead to." Doyle saw the security men and called to them. They came over and waited.

"You all have seen Larry Janin, so you know what he looks like. He's missing and needs to be found. Go out in two groups of two men, for safety, and see if you can find him. You know most of the hiding places on the island. Be careful and if you find him, shoot a rifle shot in the air, twice. I'll see if we can find you. Fire again after ten minutes. Now go and be careful."

The men broke into two groups and ran off after plotting their search. "If any other man gets shot or killed, other than Janin, I'm going to shoot him myself." Doyle turned to Poppy. "I'm sorry, we haven't had much fun or relaxation, have we?"

"Hey, this has been fun, other than the deaths. Your life is so interesting. I think I'll keep you," she giggled.

"Thank you, my dear, I appreciate that." Doyle heard a bell ringing. It signified that food was being served. "Well, I could use something to eat. Shall we go?"

Doyle's Paradise

They walked to the building where the food tables were set up. People were gathering and taking food from the bowls and trays, heaping it onto plates. Marge and Lorna came in and went up to Doyle.

"Food's on," Marge said cheerfully and went to the tables. Lorna moved slower than the older woman, but managed to get her food.

The four of them sat at a table and ate, while Doyle was looking around the room at the people talking and eating.

After twenty minutes, David came rushing in and over to Doyle. "Mr. Doyle, you need to come with me," he said breathlessly. Doyle stood, followed by Poppy.

"Enjoy your food, Marge. See you later." They followed David out and went through the jungle on a beaten path. "What's up?" Doyle called to the energetic young man.

"You'll see," was all he said.

They went through a passageway in the tall rocks that came out to the beach. The man stopped and said, "That path is the only way to get to this part of the beach, other than by the water." The other three men were standing by the water as Doyle, Poppy and David approached.

David pointed out to the water. They could see a tiny dot in the distance. "What is it?" Doyle asked.

"It's Janin and someone else. We came out here just as they were moving away from land. We could tell it was Janin," one of the men said. "We don't know who the other person was."

"You should have shot them, but I understand." He figured the men had never shot a human and didn't want to start now. "Did the other man bring him the boat?"

"He must have. He must have had help getting it here, it's too small of a boat to take from the big island. We didn't see the man sail in."

"Maybe they have a larger ship out in the distance. If so, why didn't they just sail in and pick him up?" Poppy asked.

"They didn't want to be seen, probably," Doyle said. "Well, he's on his way. I should call the Coast Guard and let them know a murderer is sailing somewhere into the islands."

"The Navy also patrols the islands," said one of the men.

Doyle looked at him and said, "Do you know how to reach them?"

Doyle's Paradise

"Sure, my brother is a Naval officer on the patrols."

"Does he have a cell phone?"

"He does."

Doyle handed him the satellite phone and said to call him. The man looked at the phone and said, "The battery warning light is flashing."

"Damn, I didn't think about charging the thing. Make a quick call before it dies."

The man dialed and talked to his brother. He explained the situation and smiled. He hung up and said, "My brother said they would patrol a line from this island to the main island and stop any ships."

The man handed the phone back to Doyle. He shut it off and said to Poppy, "We need to find the charger. I don't want to be cut off again." He turned to the men and thanked them for their hard work. "Go relax and get some food. I think we can take it easy now that Janin is off the island."

Doyle and Poppy went to their bungalow and went in. The place was tossed. "What the hell?" Doyle uttered. There were clothes scattered, and the luggage was on the floor. The bed was torn apart and the drawers on the dresser were all pulled out.

Bob Moats

"I hope you hid the papers well," Doyle said.

Poppy picked up a tampon box from the floor, still unopened. She pulled on the side and it opened up. "It's a special box I made for just such occasions. She pulled out the papers and handed them to Doyle. "I don't need tampons, but the box comes in handy. No man wants to mess with them."

Doyle laughed aloud and kissed her, giving her a big hug. "You're right, I would never have found them in that." Doyle moved around the room checking on personal property. "Doesn't look like he took anything else. He just wanted the papers."

They took a few minutes, straightening their articles. Doyle found the charger in Kabe's stuff and plugged it in. "Okay, we can relax now. Hopefully we can spend the rest of the week enjoying paradise."

"I hope I can relax. We still have to deal with the two bodies in the cooler," Poppy said.

"You're just a killjoy, aren't you? I'll have Doc call the island and have someone pick them up. Then I'll have to endure the police questioning about what happened. I'm sure they'll suspect us, they always do. At least we are on an island in international waters, so they can't arrest us," Doyle joked.

Doyle's Paradise

They got the bungalow back to the way it was and went to the door. Marge and Lorna were just going to their bungalow. "Marge, did you two get your fill?"

"Yes, Arthur, it was good and I'm full," she replied.

"Lorna, may I talk to you?"

The woman nodded and waited for Doyle and Poppy to approach. Marge waited with Lorna.

"Just so you know, the man we suspect who murdered your husband has left the island. The Navy is searching for him on the ocean. Hopefully they will find him and hold him until the police can get there to question him. Whatever, he's gone, so please try and relax now."

Marge came to her and said, "I'll take care of her. She can relax with me."

*

Chapter 20

"Thanks, Marge. The two of you have some fun now. I'm sure the danger is over," Doyle said.

He took Poppy by the hand and led her to the beach. "You know we still haven't found the nude beach," he said.

"No one has been down here to our beach other than Marge and Lorna. If we warn them to stay away we can get naked." Poppy said.

"I think we'll do that later, I just want to relax and watch the sun go down."

"As you wish," she replied.

They sat on the beach and watched the sun slowly sink into the ocean. "I wonder if the Navy found Janin yet?"

"You needed to think of that right now? This is romantic or don't you have a romantic bone in your body?"

"I can be romantic," he defended.

"Yes, in bed. But what about in the daylight?"

Doyle's Paradise

Doyle was silent. He looked out at the ocean and sighed. "I'm sorry. I had a great romantic relationship with my late wife. As I've told you, she died in a car crash and my life ended there. I didn't get over it till years later, when I started to see women again. Mostly for making out in bed. Not exactly romantic. I just couldn't get my feelings back up. I was numb about romance, but I thought that I had it back a couple times recently with a few women, but crime always reared its ugly head and ruined what I had started. You were the first woman who had some experience in crime investigating to ignore the problems I have in coming across murder and mayhem. I'm just now getting used to you and the fact that you tolerate what I do. So forgive me if I'm slow in being romantic."

She put her head on his shoulder and said, "I like your lifestyle. I know how to handle crime and crooked people, and I see you do too. I'm not a soft, gentle woman, I'm tough and yet I have feelings. I think you understand that and tolerate me, too."

"Just don't shoot me in your sleep," Doyle said with a laugh and pulled her back to the ground, kissing her passionately.

They made out until it was dark and they heard Marge calling to them.

"What's wrong, Marge?" Doyle yelled back to her.

"Just wanted to know you two are all right," she called back.

"Oh, we're just fine now, thanks. Go to bed or whatever," Doyle yelled to her. "Is Lorna still with you?"

"No, she decided to go back to her bungalow. I walked her there and came back. I had my gun with me," she replied.

"You didn't shoot anyone?"

"No, the guests are safe. Good night."

Doyle and Poppy lay back on the grass looking up at the millions of stars. "That's something you don't see in the city," Poppy said.

"No lights out here to block the star shine. It is beautiful," Doyle said quietly.

They got up and went back to their bungalow. They undressed, crashed on the bed and cuddled. "I'm beat, shall we call it a night?" Doyle asked.

"I'm fine with that." She kissed his cheek and turn on her side, spooning Doyle.

Doyle's Paradise

They slept well for the first time since they got there.

~~*~~

Oscar was up and dressed to go pick up Kent Simmons at the airport's commercial terminals. He wanted to leave early because he didn't know how long it would take to find the terminal. He was going to drive his car out from his childhood home after kissing his mother good morning and telling her a little white lie. "I'm going to look up some old friends in the city, I'll be back later."

"Don't get killed," she said in her motherly way.

"Ma, I have my gun with me," he replied with a grin.

"So, don't go shooting yourself, then," she scolded him.

"Yeah, ma, thanks," he kissed her cheek and left quickly.

He drove over to JFK Airport and managed to find the right terminal. He pulled up and saw Kent standing by a building with a carry-on bag. Kent waved and went to Oscar's car. He got in and Oscar drove back out.

"I arranged a room at the Marriott Hotel for you. Have you talked to Doyle since we last spoke?"

"He called me early this morning when he got up and asked if I could look up the name of his suspect in the murders."

"Did he catch him?"

"No, he escaped and is being sought. I ran his name through our databases and came up with interesting facts about Larry Janin. Seems he has a record for numerous aggravated assaults and attempted murder. He beat the system with high-paid lawyers, which I think are connected to New York Heavy Equipment and Sales."

"Did you check on the company?"

"I did and they have no record of being on the radar for tax evasion, or anything else for that matter. They came out clean. Now I did find out through tax records that Janin was being paid by the company. So he's on their payroll. Nice to have a hitman working for a crooked company. Have you located the company offices?"

"I drove by there last night and scoped it out. It's nothing fancy, just a plain building with a large display room of smaller construction equipment. The fenced in yard on the side had larger equipment, forklifts, cranes and front loaders. Stuff like that. I can't see how a company like that would be able to cheat the tax man?"

The construction business is huge. Lots of heavy equipment is needed and sales can go into the millions. Especially if they're selling to the government."

"The government? What would they do with cranes and bulldozers?"

"They send them overseas to third world countries for building their economies back up. Lots of government contractors are making millions plowing down war torn cities and rebuilding. I talked to my SAIC and explained the whole thing to him. He gave me full authorization to investigate. He also said to bring in Treasury agents if need be. I just wish Doyle could get me the papers that Kabe kept regarding the corruption."

"Does FedEX pick up and deliver to the island?"

Kent laughed and said, "I seriously doubt it. So take me to the company and let's see what we can find out."

They drove to the building in an industrial section of the city. As Oscar said, nothing fancy. "I guess they don't want to attract much attention," Oscar said.

"They probably have a built-in clientele list, so they don't need sales off the street," Kent said. "I do see they have guards in the parking lot, strange for a sales company."

"Maybe they don't want the street gangs stealing a backhoe to dig into a convenience store," Oscar said with a laugh. Kent agreed.

Oscar pulled into a parking lot across the street from the company parking. "So let's talk about what you know, so far." Oscar asked.

Kent took out a note pad with names of the company officers and employees. "We need to talk to the head of accounting, Dimone Hanjoi. If we hit them where they hide the books, we may shake them up."

*

Chapter 21

Oscar pulled out of the parking lot and went across the street to the company parking lot. He stopped at the gate when a very big, tall, bald black man with scars across his cheek stepped out to stop them. He leaned down to ask, "What do you need?"

Oscar looked at Kent and said, "That didn't sound very friendly." He turned back to the guard and said, "We need to see Mr. Hanjoi, please."

"Do you have an appointment?" he said, growling.

"No, we don't," Oscar replied.

"Well, I can't let you in," he said abruptly.

Kent leaned over and brought his badge up. "I'm Special Agent Simmons, FBI, and I need your name."

The guard stiffened and asked, "Why?"

"Well, you're impeding a criminal investigation. I may need to get a warrant for your arrest and I like to know who to blame."

The guard stiffened more and said, "Okay, you can go in." He stepped back and went into the guard shack.

"That badge works well, where can I get one?" Oscar asked.

"Lots of places, just don't get caught using it for official business."

Oscar drove in and parked in a space at the side of the building. They got out and went in. They found a counter in the wall by the door and a woman stood, opening the sliding glass partition.

"May I help you gentlemen?" she asked.

"We'd like to see Mr. Hanjoi, please," Kent asked.

"Do you have an appointment?" she asked.

Kent looked at Oscar, smiled and handed him the badge. Oscar grinned and held the badge out. "FBI, we're investigating a crime and we need to see Hanjoi. Where would we find him?"

The woman looked surprised and said, "I'll call him to let him now you're here."

"No," Kent said. "Just point us to his office and we'll find him, please."

Doyle's Paradise

"Uh, okay, down this hall, the last door on the right. Are you sure you don't want me to call him?"

"No, thanks. We'll surprise him," Kent said and the men went down the hall to the door. The name on the door said 'Accounting' and they went in.

There were three desks lined along a wall, with only two men at those desks. They looked at the two men entering the room and the man at the closest desk stood and said, "Do you belong in here?"

"I don't know, are you Dimone Hanjoi?" Kent asked. The man was thin, looked to be Arabic.

The man expressed surprise and said, "I am. Who are you?"

Kent pulled out his badge again and said, "FBI. I'm Special Agent Kent Simmons and this is Oscar Drew. We're here to investigate the murder of Elmer Kabe."

The man stumbled slightly and sat back in his chair. "Oh, my God. Elmer was murdered? When? Where?"

Kent pulled a chair over next to Hanjoi and straddled it backward. Oscar sat on the other side of the desk, surrounding Hanjoi. "Talk to me Dimone, what do you know about his murder?" Kent blurted.

He got very wide-eyed. "Me? I haven't the faintest idea about this. I hardly knew Kabe. He came in here often to drop off contracts for us to file. He never spoke much."

"Well, it seems that Kabe had records about double deals and faked billings. You were cooking the books weren't you, Dimone?"

The man was flapping his mouth like a bass fish and having trouble breathing. "No, it wasn't me. I didn't want to be involved, but they made me look away or I would be a dead man, they said. Another accountant handled the real books and I was to make the entries of sales that they provided to me in the books for the tax people. I knew this would bite me in the ass," he moaned.

"Okay, Dimone, if you testify about the tax fraud we can keep you from the murder investigation. I'm sure you wouldn't have wanted Kabe murdered."

"No, no, I wouldn't. I didn't know they did this. Where was Mr. Kabe murdered?"

"On an island in the Pacific. Do you know a man named Larry Janin?"

"Janin? I've seen his name in the pay ledgers. He makes a ton of money off this company."

Doyle's Paradise

"Well, we believe he was the killer of Kabe. What do you think of that?"

"Agent Simmons, I have no idea. I just deal with numbers and I'm ashamed to say the numbers aren't what they should be."

"Okay, I'm calling for Federal Marshals to come and take you into protective custody. This company is responsible for the murder of Kabe. You could be next."

That struck a chord with the man. "I need to be protected. I can give you the books that show they cheated on their taxes, for millions."

Kent looked at Oscar and smiled. "Yes, we'll protect you. Can you get the files?"

"I can download them onto a flash drive. They're all in the computer, in password protected files. I know the passwords."

"Do that, Dimone." Kent said, looked at Oscar, motioned to him to stand and follow him. They went nearby, as Dimone was working the computer. "I wonder why Kabe didn't have his damaging evidence on a flash drive. Why paper?"

"As I understand it, Kabe was a lawyer. Maybe they like to work with paper, so they don't have to lug around a laptop all day."

Kent smiled and said, "You know Oscar, if you get tired of working for Doyle, I could find a job for you at the Bureau."

"Nah, I like working with Doyle. His lifestyle is interesting."

The accountant said he was finished and handed the flash drive to Kent.

"Write down your home address, then leave now and go there. I'll have Marshals come to provide you protection."

Hanjoi's head was bobbing up and down as he sat and wrote his address. He handed the slip of paper to Kent and stood.

"Good man, now get away from here, fast. Before the company knows you gave us this information."

"They shouldn't know unless you tell them, right?" he asked.

"They won't hear it from us, but when the IRS agents come in, they'll know you and Kabe had something to do with it. They will need you to testify also. Now, you can follow us out so we can watch you leave safely."

Doyle's Paradise

Hanjoi looked at the other man who was minding his own business at his computer. He nodded his head and followed the men out.

In the parking lot, they parted after Kent told him to go home and wait. They watched the man nervously enter his car and he quickly drove out of the parking lot.

"I hope he doesn't have an accident driving home," Oscar said, grinning.

"I'll call the Federal Marshals and explain that he's going to be a witness in the tax evasion case. They can do what they want with him now."

"What do we do now?" Oscar asked.

"Well, you can show me around New York. I've been here once before, but never got to enjoy my stay."

"I can do that. I know a couple good bars that we can visit. Think we should call Doyle and let him know what we have?"

"Ah, let's let him stew a bit. I don't want him to relax too much in paradise." Kent grinned and they got in the car.

*

Chapter 22

Doyle was standing over Poppy as she was lying out on the grass above the beach. She turned her head to him and asked, "Are you going to go into the water or just stand there making shade over me?"

"I already told you, I don't swim with sharks. I'm going to see what Marge is up to. I feel bad leaving her all alone."

"She likes her solitude. I think Lorna was getting on her nerves."

"Well, Lorna has gone back to her bungalow and I'm going to see what Marge is up to. I'll be back," he said and went back up the path to Marge's bungalow. Marge was sitting on her porch with a book, reading. She looked up and saw Doyle coming towards her.

"Arthur, I thought you were relaxing by the water?" she asked.

"I was, but I was concerned that you were getting bored."

Doyle's Paradise

"Arthur, I sit all day in your office while you and Oscar are running around chasing crime. I'm alone and I enjoy it. As long as I have my music and my knitting or a good book, I'm happy." She held up the MP3 player and showed Doyle the earphones were in her ears.

"Good, Marge, I'm glad you can amuse yourself. Have you heard from Lorna?"

"I hardly heard from her when she was staying with me. She kept going off saying she wanted to get fresh air or take a walk. I'd say half the time I was watching her, I didn't see her."

"Oh, really. What times was she gone?"

"Let's see," she thought about it. "The first time was the day before yesterday, she said she was going to the office to ask if she could leave the island. Of course, they told her no. Then she went out that same night, she said she wanted to watch the stars from the beach. I told her I could go with her, but she said no. That was the night Morris got shot. Then she was gone for an hour yesterday, around the time that hit man's wife was killed," Marge paused, now looking concerned.

"Yeah, I was thinking the same thing. You don't know if she has a gun?"

"I never saw her with one, but I never examined her purse."

"Maybe Elmer brought a gun with him. He was fearing for his life, and he smuggled a sat phone with him, so why not a gun?"

"Why would we think that she may have killed anyone?"

"Well, Janin wouldn't murder his companion, so who would have done that? It's something that has bothered me."

"You think Lorna found out that her husband's secretary was on the island and she blamed her for her husband's death?"

"Good thinking, Marge. I may need to go see her," Doyle said as he felt someone come up behind him. He jumped and turned to see Poppy.

"What's gotten into you?" she asked.

"I'm starting to believe that Lorna may have been a killer, also."

"I knew from her beady little eyes that she was a bad guy," Poppy said with a smile.

"Seriously, didn't you find it strange that Janice Wall was murdered in their bungalow?"

Doyle's Paradise

"I figured Janin did it. They weren't married and we suspected Janin brought her here to cover him being the hitman. Maybe he wanted to get away clean and didn't want to drag her along."

"Well, that does make sense. But since he escaped from the island, why would he care if he left her here."

"To cover loose ends. She could give the authorities testimony as to the murder of Kabe by the company and definite proof that Janin did it. But I can see why you'd think Lorna could have murdered Janice, to avenge her husband."

"Now you're casting reasonable doubt as to Lorna's involvement. But I think we still need to ask her about her activities the last couple days. Marge said she wandered off a lot."

"Can't hurt to talk. Let me get dressed and we'll go hunt her down," Poppy said and went over to the bungalow.

Doyle turned back to Marge and asked, "What was her state of mind the last couple days?"

"Actually, she did seem awfully calm. Almost too calm for a newlywed who became a newly widowed. Although, she seemed upset after she got back yesterday, just before you found the Wall woman dead."

"That makes me wonder." Doyle turned back to the path when he heard someone coming. It was David, the security officer. "Good morning, David."

"Good morning, Mr. Doyle. Have you heard anything more about Albert?" the young man asked.

"No, I need to get the phone to Doc and let him call. I'll do that shortly, I have to go question Kabe's wife."

"Mrs Kabe? I saw her going into the jungle on the trail about five minutes ago, as I was coming here."

"Did she have anything with her?"

"Just a large purse."

"Thanks, David. Hang on and you can go with us to find her. You know the trails better than I do."

Poppy came out of the bungalow and greeted David.

"Good morning, ma'am," David said.

Doyle's Paradise

She grinned at his reference of ma'am, it made her sound old. "Call me Miss Drake, not ma'am."

"Sorry, I was raised to respect women. In the South, we call all women ma'am."

"Good upbringing. Too bad the Northerners don't have the same respect," she said looking at Doyle.

"Hey, I respect women," Doyle defended.

She went to him, kissed his cheek and whispered in his ear, "Sure, you respect women in bed."

Doyle frowned and said, "Shall we go find Lorna?"

They went back on the path, after Doyle told Marge to enjoy herself. David led them to where he saw Lorna going into the jungle.

"I haven't noticed, are there any monkeys on this island?" Poppy asked David as they made their way through the bush.

"No, the last monkey was a pet of one of the staff. But he got into too much trouble, so Mr. Dante said he had to go. There are no wild monkeys here."

"Mostly birds, I see. Any other wildlife?" she asked.

"None, this island doesn't have much in the way of animals. Most couldn't swim the distance from the big island," he said with a grin.

"Now you're messing with me," Poppy laughed.

David grinned and kept going. Doyle followed up the rear and was watching out for Lorna.

They kept going for about a mile when they came to a clearing overlooking the ocean. It was a cliff with a railing to prevent people from falling over the edge. They saw Lorna standing looking out at the water. She turned her head to them and smiled.

"Good morning," she said as they came up. "My, everyone looks so serious. Was there another murder?"

"No, it's been quiet since Janin left," Doyle said. "Lorna, I have to ask, do you or Elmer own a gun?"

She showed no expression and said, "Elmer had one, but he left it back home in New York. I don't think he brought it with him. Why?"

"Lorna, did you know that Janice Wall was on the island before she was shot?"

She was silent for a moment then said, "I'm getting the idea that you suspect me of her murder. Am I correct?"

Chapter 23

"I'm not accusing you, but it seems strange that Janin would murder her. If he didn't, then who would have a reason to do it? You did say she was the person who knew you and Elmer were going to be here. It would be her doing that brought Janin here to murder Elmer. Did Elmer know she was here? You all came over on the same plane, why didn't he see her?"

"If he had, he didn't say. I didn't know what she looked like, but Elmer worked with her, so he would have known. As I said, he never mentioned it to me, so maybe he never saw her. She could have been disguised."

"Do you mind if I look in your purse?" Doyle asked.

"I do mind," she replied quietly.

"Lorna, we're not in the United State here. I've been given the authority to be in charge of the island in Dante's absence and David here, as a security officer, is as close to island police as it gets. Now we can be friendly about this and you can let me see in your bag."

156

She hesitated and looked around, stalling. She took the purse and started to hand it to him, but she tossed it over the edge of the cliff. David and Doyle went to the railing and looked down. Luckily the purse landed on a small patch of shore close to the lapping water.

"I can get down there, I know a way," David said.

"Do it, before the tide gets it." Doyle replied as David ran off. "Lorna, that only makes you look guilty. What was in the purse? The gun?"

She said nothing. Poppy went to her and took her arm. "You'll need to come back with us."

She didn't argue, just went with them. They went back to the compound and found the doctor outside the main office.

"Good morning, Doyle and company. I hope you all slept well?" he asked.

Doyle handed him the satellite phone and said, "We did. Can you call to see how Albert is doing? Is there somewhere we can lock up Mrs. Kabe?"

"Lock her up, why?"

Doyle's Paradise

"Long story, I'll fill you in later," he said as he saw one of the security officers coming around the building. "I'll ask him, just call the hospital, please."

The officer was the same man who was related to the Naval officer who was chasing Janin. "What's your name?" he asked as the man came up.

"Brian, sir."

"Brian, I'll need you to help us lock up this woman. Do you have a place?"

"We have a small jail cell for men who get overly drunk."

"Good, lead the way," he said and told the doctor he'd be back for the phone.

They went to the security building and in to the back where there was a small cell with a barred door. Brian opened the cell and Poppy escorted Lorna in. The door was locked and Doyle said, "I'm sorry, Lorna. Bad enough your husband was murdered but this doesn't help. When you feel up to it, you'll need to talk."

They went back out to the front office. Doyle asked, "If I bring you the phone can you call your brother in the Navy and see if they found our suspect?"

"Sure. What do I do about the woman?" he asked.

"Just let her rest and get her some food when it's served. I'll get you the phone."

Doyle and Poppy left the building, followed by Brian, and went around to the doctor's clinic. The doctor was on the porch talking on the phone. They waited for him to finish.

"Albert is coming around. Luckily, the bullet didn't do much damage. The police said the bullet was a .22 and they are examining it. I gave Dante the other bullet from Kabe, before he left, so they can compare the two. Dante is staying another day or two until they have some answers. He said he doesn't want the police to intrude on the island, but they have to get the two bodies we have. So we may have more visitors than we need. They're coming back on a Coast Guard chopper to take the bodies and bring the cops."

"I'm going to have Brian call his relative to see if they caught Janin. We'll put the blame on him, so the cops don't bother us too much," Doyle said with a grin.

"Sounds like a plan. Now why did you want to lock up Kabe's wife?"

Doyle's Paradise

"As I said, it's a long story. First, I need to find out if they found Janin, then call back to New York to my partner and see what they came up with. I'll get back to you," he said and took the phone, taking it back to Brian standing nearby.

Brian placed the call and when he finished he told Doyle the news. "Seems they found more than they were looking for. They got Janin, but they also got a boat full of guns and weapons. It was part of a gun-running operation. They never would have stopped the boat if they weren't looking for Janin."

"Glad to oblige. What are they going to do with Janin?"

"He's being turned over to Honolulu police and they are contacting Dante at the hospital for more information. This is coming together now. How's Albert doing?"

"He's out of the woods, hopefully he'll be back before long. Okay, keep an eye on the woman, I'll check back on her later."

Doyle took the phone back, then he and Poppy went to a bench in front of the main office and sat.

Doyle dialed Oscar and waited. "I need to get one of these."

"You never leave the country, why bother?"

Doyle was just about to answer when he heard Oscar. "Hey, Oscar. How's it going between you and Kent?"

"We raided the company and got some pretty juicy information. Kent is turning it over to the IRS and the Treasury Department. They can take it over now. As for your murdered lawyer, Kent said he'd look into that in a couple days. He's having too much fun in New York."

"Don't you corrupt him, the Feds need him. I have a lot more information on our mess here in paradise. I'll get with you and Kent when we get back in a couple days. I think we may try and head out early. I've had enough of paradise. Why don't you and Kent meet us in Honolulu and we can relax there?"

"That sounds like a winner. I'm getting tired of my family already. My brother won't speak to me, my mother is being too motherly and the rest of the family is getting real annoying. I think I would have had more fun in paradise."

"I'm sure you would have. I wish you had come with us, but it was good for you to see your family again, just for one more time."

"Yes, and it's the last time. I'll visit my mother occasionally, but the rest of them can just jump in the Hudson River."

"Tell Kent I said hello and see if he can get you both out here to Hawaii?"

"I will, maybe see you soon."

*

Chapter 24

Doyle finished the call and clicked off the phone. "Oscar and Kent may come out to meet us in Honolulu."

"Are we staying in paradise?"

"Yes, but not on this island. I think I would have rather had the mad scientist transplanting heads. We'll go back to the big island and stay there for a couple days. If Oscar can come out, we'll stay longer."

"I hope Marge will like that."

"Like what?" Marge said coming up behind them.

She sat on the bench next to Poppy. "As soon as we can get away from this island, we are going to Honolulu and visit."

"Ah, civilization, with television and lots of people," Marge exclaimed.

"Glad you approve, Marge," Doyle said. "We found Lorna. She's in the island's jail now."

"Arthur, you don't think she's a cold-blooded killer, do you?"

"Not really, I think she's just a frustrated woman who lost her husband to murder and decided to do away with the killer. As soon as we can see in her purse, we'll know."

On cue, David came walking up, his pants wet.

"Did you have to fish it out?" Doyle asked.

"Almost. In order to get to that part of the beach, I had to go through water. But I got it." He proudly held up the purse and handed it to Doyle.

"Did you get curious and look inside?" Doyle asked him.

Doyle's Paradise

"I didn't want to disturb the evidence," David said.

"Good man," Doyle said and opened the purse. He rummaged around inside and then carefully brought out a .22 caliber handgun. "I'd say we found the gun that killed Janice Wall. Shall we go talk to Lorna?"

They stood and went back to the security office. Marge said she'd like to watch, so she went in with them. Doyle asked David to bring Lorna out to the front office and to a table in the room. He went off with Brian and they brought Lorna out. Doyle had arranged chairs around the table for Lorna, Poppy and him. Marge sat on a chair by the door. David and Brain stood at the door next to Marge.

Doyle brought up the purse. Lorna eyed it and made a frown. He reached in and carefully brought out the gun. He turned to David and asked if he had a plastic bag. David understood and went to get one. He handed it to Doyle and he put the gun in the bag.

"Lorna, I don't think you're a murderer by nature. I think you fell into a situation that made it hard for you not to take action. Talk to me about this gun."

Lorna was tearing up. Marge took a tissue from her bag and held it out to Lorna.

Bob Moats

"I saw Janice walking with that man to their bungalow. I had seen Janice once before so I knew what she looked like. On the plane over she had to have had on a wide brimmed hat and sunglasses. This time she wasn't covering her face. I waited outside until Janin came out and went somewhere. I went to the bungalow and entered. She was in the bathroom and I saw the gun on a table. I picked it up and went to her. She looked shocked and asked who I was."

She paused and asked for water. David went to get it and brought a bottle to her. "I told her who I was and that she murdered my husband. She said it was Janin, she just came along to give Janin a cover for not being alone on the island. Make him look respectable. I moved closer to her with the gun and threatened her with telling the police. She lunged at me, we fought and she pulled my hands up. The gun went off, hitting her in the head and she fell down. I panicked and ran out, still holding on to the gun."

"Why didn't you come and tell me?" Doyle asked. "I'd say it was self-defense."

"I couldn't think, but I felt better knowing she was dead. I was going to throw the gun off the cliff, but you came before I could."

"If you found this gun in Janin's bungalow, it's probably the one that shot your husband."

She looked shocked and said, "I…I didn't think about that."

"Well, I'm sure this will be all straightened out soon. They caught Janin and once the police talk to you, they'll determine what to do with you. I'm sure we can vouch for you."

"Thank you," she said quietly.

"If I let you go free on the island, you won't go doing anything stupid? Or should we lock you back up?'

"Mr. Doyle, I promise I won't do anything stupid. Thank you."

Doyle looked back to Marge, "Think you could keep an eye on her?"

"She won't get out of my sight," Marge said. "If she runs, I'll shoot her."

"You stick close to Marge, you hear. We have a day or two before the police arrive with Dante, then we have to sit down and straighten out this mess."

"I will," Lorna said.

Everyone stood and went out of the building. The sun was shining and a warm breeze came in from the ocean.

Marge took Lorna down the path to her bungalow. Doyle could hear Marge ask if Lorna knew how to play poker. That made him laugh. He and Poppy stood in the middle of the big yard in front of the main offices. It was where the last helicopter landed and would be where the Coast Guard chopper would land.

"We haven't had much time to really relax, have we?" Poppy asked.

"Nope, I'll make up for it. We have to wait now for Dante and the police to come charging in, then endure questioning from cops who don't have jurisdiction here. Unless Dante gives it to them. I hope not. But it would be nice to have all this mess on a report for the record. We have Janin to go to trial for murder, so there has to be a report on him. I don't know what the Honolulu police are like, I hope they're friendly."

"Do you think they'll bring Janin back here for questioning?"

"Good question, since most of the evidence and murders happened here," Doyle said. "We don't have much proof that Janin did actually kill Kabe. The hand gun hopefully will have his prints on it and the bullets that were pulled from Kabe and Albert came from that gun. It's the only tie to him."

"It's good that we stopped Lorna from throwing it into the ocean," Poppy observed.

"Yes, very good. Now I don't see any more murders happening, so shall we go rest on the beach?"

"I'm right beside you."

~~*~~

Kent was just coming out of the restroom at the bar where he and Oscar were relaxing, when his cell phone buzzed. He answered and listened to someone on the other end. He was still listening as he sat across from Oscar at the table. He had a concerned look, then hung up.

"What's up, you look annoyed?" Oscar asked Kent.

"I am annoyed. That was the U.S. Marshal's office. They went to pick up Hanjoi and he didn't answer his door, they went in and found him dead. Shot in the head."

*

Chapter 25

"Oh, crap. That's not good," Oscar exclaimed.

"I was thinking stronger words. No, it's not good for Hanjoi. He didn't deserve this. I didn't figure he would be found out so quickly," Kent said.

"You had the guard at the gate, the receptionist and that other guy in the accounting office, who all knew we were there. It didn't take much to figure out why we were there. But if Janin was the hitman on their payroll, who shot Hanjoi?"

"I think we need to find out. First, we have to take the flash drive we have to the Federal building and turn it into the tax people. Let's stir these government idiots up into raiding New York Heavy Equipment and Sales."

"I'm with you, shall we go?"

They went back out into the heat of the city and to Oscar's car. "I haven't any idea where the new Federal building is. They changed it from when I lived here."

"Hold on," Kent said and placed a call on his cell phone. "This is Special Agent Kent Simmons, Detroit

FBI. I need the location of your offices." He listened and told Oscar the directions. "Thanks." He hung up and asked, "Do you know the area?"

"I do, I hear it's a newly developed area. Lots of new buildings that replaced centuries old buildings and shops. The price of progress." Oscar started the car and drove out.

They arrived and pulled into a parking structure. They went to the main entrance and found guards at the door manning the metal detector grids. Kent held out his badge and they checked it. "This man is with me, he's a good guy," he said pointing to Oscar.

They let them through, after Kent asked where the FBI Bureau offices were. They gave him directions and he thanked them.

They went up to the second floor and Kent found a desk where there stood a big agent. He eyed them and Kent pulled his badge again. "Special Agent Kent Simmons, Detroit FBI Division. I need to see the SAIC."

"Do you have an appointment?" he asked.

Kent sighed, "I have evidence of murder and corruption involving government sales through a local company. Do you think he may excuse the lack of an appointment for a big bust involving millions of dollars?"

The man stood motionless, then picked up a phone. He made a call and said something into it. He hung up and said "The Special Agent In Charge will see you."

"Thank you. Can you direct us to the office?"

The man gave them directions and they went there.

The girl in the reception room made a phone call and then told them to go in.

The man in the room stood and came around the desk. "Agent Simmons, I was expecting you. Your boss called me and said to give you my cooperation on your case. Please come and sit." He pointed to the chairs and went back around his desk. "Now, I understand you're investigating a murder involving a lawyer from a company here in New York?"

"That and corruption in tax reporting by that company. We just had another murder today here in New York involving the company's accounting department head. We managed to get a flash drive with the cooked books that the IRS will be interested in seeing. The man who gave us the evidence was shot in the head while he waited for Marshals to come and protect him. I feel I screwed up in letting him go home alone. I want blood now."

Doyle's Paradise

The SAIC smiled and said, "I'm sorry that you had an unfortunate incident. I'll call and get the IRS forensic people to look at the flash drive and if they find evidence of corruption, we'll be more than happy to take the company down. What is the name of the company?"

"New York Heavy Equipment and Sales," he replied.

The man looked at Kent and said, "Really? We've had word that they are connected with organized crime. I'll have to relay this to OCU. Looks like we may nail them all around."

Kent gave the flash drive to the SAIC and they finished up. Oscar and Kent went back to their car and sat.

"This isn't going to help Hanjoi, but maybe make his contribution worth it," Kent said.

"What about Kabe? He started this whole thing rolling. He deserves some thanks, too."

"I agree. Speaking of paradise and murder, you did say Doyle wanted us to meet him in Honolulu, correct?"

"He did ask that. I think if we are going to properly investigate this case, we need to go to the source," Oscar said trying not to smile.

"Well, we need to get moving. Can you leave your family on such short notice?"

"I was ready to leave them yesterday. We'll need to drive back to Detroit to drop my car off and you can check in with your people."

"Why are you still sitting here? My bags are in the car, shall we get yours?"

"My ma is going to be upset and want you to stay for dinner. Resist her at all cost."

"I can do that," Kent said with a grin.

Oscar drove back to his modest little home on a street where the houses all looked the same. He pulled up to the curb and said, "Resist her at all cost, or we'll never get out of here."

"Why don't I wait in the car?" Kent said.

"I need you as proof that I have to leave early, or I'll never get away clean."

"Okay, lead the way."

They exited the car and went in the house. "Ma? Where are you?"

Doyle's Paradise

Mrs. Drew came out of the kitchen wiping her hands on a towel. "Oscar, you brought home a friend, how nice. Can he stay for dinner?"

"No, Ma. I have to go back to Detroit now. This is Special Agent Kent Simmons, from the FBI in Detroit and I'm needed back in Detroit. It's a murder case that we have to solve." He didn't totally lie to her.

"Oh, how terrible. Well, I hope you catch the killer," she replied.

"Thanks Ma. I have to get my bags and go now. I'll call you when I get there."

"Nice to meet you Mrs. Drew. Sorry for the rush, but we have to get on this quickly."

Ten minutes later, they were on the road. "Nice lady, your mom," Kent said with a smile.

"Yeah, but you never had to live with her," Oscar said with a laugh.

Nine hours later they hit the border of Michigan. "I'll take you to my place and we can catch a cab to your office."

"I'll charter the Bureau's jet to take us to Honolulu. I have to convince my boss that the trip is needed, but I think I have justifiable cause." He hoped.

Ninety minutes later, they were at the commercial hangers at Metro Airport south of Detroit waiting to fly away to Paradise.

"This is happening so fast. I need to call Doyle and tell him where we are." Oscar pulled out his cell phone and called. He heard Doyle answer and said to him, "Put on a couple extra dinner plates, you got company coming."

*

Chapter 26

"When do you think you'll arrive in Honolulu?" Doyle paused to listen. "I don't know how soon we'll be able to leave the island. We have to wait for the police to arrive and grill us, then take the two bodies back to Honolulu. Can you catch a flight to our island?" He paused again. "Good, call when you get into Honolulu and I'll explain the rest. Talk later." He hung up and turned to Poppy sitting next to him on the bench.

Doyle's Paradise

"Oscar and Kent are winging their way to paradise. They have a long flight from Detroit, but they're on one of the FBI's private jets so they won't have to endure TSA inspections. Plus the jet moves faster than commercial airplanes so they may have a shorter flight."

"They can sleep on the beach, I'm not sharing my bungalow with anyone else," Poppy said firmly.

"Maybe we can put them in with Marge. She's running a boarding house now."

"She should charge bed and breakfast rates. Speaking of breakfast, we haven't eaten yet. Shall we go?"

"It's after lunch time, but I think they'll have something left over."

They went to the big hall and found Marge and Lorna eating at a table. They went to get their food and sat with them.

Doyle told Marge, "Oscar and my FBI friend Kent Simmons are flying out to visit us. Kent must have bamboozled his boss into letting him come here. He always was sneaky."

"Glad that Oscar could join us. How was his visit with his family?" Marge asked.

"He didn't say, ask him when he gets here."

They finished their food and went back to the bungalow. "Lorna, it's better if you stay with Marge again. Not that I don't trust you, but you still are a suspect in the shooting of Janice Wall."

"I understand, thank you," she replied.

Everyone went down and relaxed on the beach. Marge sat on a blanket reading while Lorna waded in the water. Doyle and Poppy sat watching the ocean waves as the sun going down.

"Oscar and Kent should get in after midnight," Doyle said. "They can go bug the Honolulu FBI and the police. Maybe they can catch a ride in on the helicopter. It will be good to see Oscar again. I actually missed his help on this case."

"Hey, you had me," Poppy said indignantly.

"Yes, and you were an inspiration to me. I figure the police will roar in tomorrow morning. Dante will be able to tell us how Albert is doing. We have a lot of explaining to do. I think we need to go see David and get our facts straight." He stood, helping Poppy up. "Marge, we're going to find David and have a meeting. You two play nice."

Doyle's Paradise

She waved them off and they went back to the security office. David was standing out front when they came up.

"Mr. Doyle, have you heard anything about Albert?" he asked.

"Not since earlier today. I'm sure Mr. Dante and the police will be coming in tomorrow, so I think we need to get together and talk about the events of the last couple days."

"Okay, we can go sit in the office." They went in and spent a couple hours talking about what happened and what they found. They all agreed about going easy on Lorna, and playing down her trying to hide the gun.

"She was just frightened and misguided. She wasn't trying to be deceitful about disposing of the weapon," Poppy said. "We'll have to emphasize that."

"Okay, I think we covered everything, now to talk with the police and convince them. My friend from the FBI may have more jurisdiction than the police on this island. So maybe they will let him take lead. Let's wrap this up and go get some sleep. It should be a quiet night."

"You hope," Poppy muttered.

"Fine, you can stay up and watch for crime. I'm going to bed," Doyle said and stood. They went out after saying their good nights to David.

The two of them were walking back on the path to the bungalow, as Poppy took Doyle's hand. "This wasn't such a bad place to be, if it weren't for the murders. It was actually enjoyable."

"Yes, if it weren't for the murders."

They arrived at their bungalow and went in.

Early next morning the satellite phone was buzzing on the charger. Doyle stumbled out of bed to get it and answered. "Doyle here, who's this?" he said grumpily.

"Well, good morning to you, sunshine." It was Kent.

"Hey, are you guys in Honolulu?"

"We are and we talked to the police already. Your Mr. Dante is very excitable. I don't think he wants the police on his island and if it weren't for the murder and the bodies, from what I'm hearing, I don't think the police want to be out there either. Too far out for them to mess with."

"Well, we have to tie this up somehow. Can you get the FBI involved, since this happened in international waters?" Doyle asked.

"Jurisdiction is flaky in international waters, but if the police will let me and you pretty much have this figured out, I may be able to take it. I contacted the FBI Division in LA where the police have Janin and it turns out he's on our list of wanted men. The police just didn't know it until they took prints. The FBI has him in custody now."

"Good, if we can contain this all through the FBI, it will make things a lot simpler. What happened back in New York?"

"I'll fill you in when I get there. Dante is wanting to get back to his island, I think he's afraid the island is going to fall apart without him. So we'll be flying out in a couple hours. As soon as we get a green-light from the Coast Guard."

"Great, be good to see you again." They finished and Doyle hung up.

"Oscar and Kent are on the way?" Poppy moaned from the bed.

"In a couple hours. We need to get ready for their arrival. Kent said he thinks the police don't want to bother with this, so we may only have to contend with Kent. Now get up and let's get some food before Marge eats it all."

They entered the hall where the guests were getting their fill of food. Marge and Lorna were already eating. Doyle got his food, went to the table and sat. "Oscar and Kent are coming out. I'm hoping the police decide not to come. It will be easier for you, Lorna."

"Will Kent take lead on the investigation?" Marge asked.

"We'll see," he replied, as Poppy came and sat.

They ate their food and went out to find David. He and his men were putting the sheet with the big orange 'H' in the middle back down for the chopper to land.

Marge and Lorna went to sit on a bench as Doyle and Poppy went to David. "Glad you're on top of this. I got a call and the chopper is scheduled to arrive sometime in the next hour or two."

"Is Mr. Dante going to be with them?"

"He is and he's hot to get back. David, you did very well helping me on this. If Albert isn't able to work again, I'll tell Dante to put you in charge."

"Thank you, Mr. Doyle. I appreciate that."

They looked up when they heard a loud noise. "Well, David, I'd say we have guests," Doyle said as they saw the helicopter approaching.

*

Chapter 27

They all moved away from the center of the yard as the helicopter made one circle around the area to get oriented to the winds and the landing area. Hitting a tree would take the chopper out fast. The big Coast Guard beast landed safely and four Coast Guard officers jumped out to block the wheels and secure the blades after it wound down. Then Dante came bounding out and over to David. Doyle and Poppy waited for Oscar and Kent to get out.

Four men in combat uniforms got out, followed by a woman, Oscar and then Kent. Oscar saw Doyle and went to him. "Man, I'm glad to see you," he said as he gave Doyle a bear hug. Doyle said he was happy to see him, too.

"Now let me go, I think you're too happy." Doyle pulled back, as Oscar laughed.

"Who's the military?" Doyle asked as Kent came up.

"They're Feds with the Honolulu FBI tactical team. They're going to take charge of the bodies." Kent replied. "I managed to relieve the Honolulu police from coming out here. We'll take the bodies back to our HQ and take charge here. Dante didn't mind once I told him I was a friend of yours. I think he's hiding something he doesn't want the police to see. He's been very nervous about them coming out. He only accepted me under the agreement that I keep this a low profile."

"Two murders plus one attempted, and he wants to keep it a low profile? He has to be hiding something. So you're running the show?"

"Yep, I need to get all the pieces in place. From here to Janin in LA to New York, the case is spread all over the place. We have Janin in custody, I'll be talking to him later, now we need to get the bodies back for examination. You have the gun that shot Kabe and Morris?"

Doyle turned to Poppy as she took the plastic bag with the weapon out of her bag. She handed it to him.

Doyle's Paradise

"Good, I'll have our forensics run this against the bullets I got from the police. If you feel this is the gun that took out Kabe, I'm happy."

"Who's the woman?" Doyle asked watching the female standing by the chopper, looking lost.

"Damn, I forgot about her. She's a steno and will take down testimony." Kent yelled for her and she came over. "Everyone, this is Agent Milly Harper. She'll record all the details." They all greeted her. "I wanted everything recorded so Milly will be taking down everything we say."

Dante finished talking to David and came over to them. "Mr. Doyle, David gave me a quick run-down of what happened in my absence, thank you. I'm glad you took control and kept peace."

"My pleasure, and David did a great job helping me. You need to give him a promotion."

"I'll do that. I also need to have my security take more training to handle situations like this."

Doc Hakon came out of the clinic and over to the men. "Welcome back, Harold," he said to Dante.

"Doc, these men," Doyle said, pointing to the tactical team, "are going to take the bodies back to Honolulu to the FBI forensic labs."

"Good, the cooks were getting nervous having the bodies in the meat locker. One actually said he heard one of the bodies make a noise. I told him it was gases building up in the bodies."

"So dead bodies actually fart?" Oscar said. Everyone laughed, and Doyle introduced the doctor to the new people.

"I'll show your men to the bodies, but I don't recommend taking them out of the cooler until they are ready to go back to Honolulu," the doctor said.

Kent said to the men, "Go take a look and then just relax until we get some questions answered."

The doctor took the men to the building with the kitchens and coolers. The Coast Guard officers were relaxing around the chopper, waiting.

Kent turned back to Doyle, "We need to sit down and go over the facts. Where's a good place?"

Dante said, "We can use my conference room. It's comfortable and quiet."

"Works for me," Kent said. "Get everyone involved together and we'll go there," he told Doyle.

Doyle signaled to Marge and Lorna to follow and had David get Brian. They headed for Dante's office and went in. They waited for the doctor and he finally came in.

For the next two hours, Doyle went over the timeline for all the incidents. Agent Harper was taking notes on a portable steno machine. Kent talked to Lorna and got her testimony, then talked to Poppy to get her reaction. David explained what he did and Brian spoke briefly. Marge was finally asked to give her opinion. She gave a glowing review of Lorna and the rest of the security team.

"Okay, we've been covering the last four days. I think I've got enough to settle this. I'll file my report and then I'll close the case after I interrogate Janin and we get the results from the gun. Lorna will have to give testimony about her shooting, but I think she'll be all right. Let's break and go refresh our minds. I'd like to see what paradise is like." They stood and left the conference room.

Outside, Doyle, Oscar, Poppy, and Kent stood waiting for Marge and Lorna to come out. Dante, David, and Brian stayed in the office. Agent Harper came out after closing up her equipment.

"So, I think I have all I need to know," Kent said. "Kabe came out here to get his evidence together, but was followed by Janin and murdered by him. Albert Morris was shot because he didn't follow directions by Janin. Janice Wall was accidentally shot by Lorna, causing Janin to run from the island. But how did he contact the boat to come get him?"

"You'll have to beat it out of Janin. That puzzled me too," Doyle said.

"I've got most of the Feds attacking New York Heavy Equipment and Sales. They will have to do some real explaining about their tax obligation and connection to the murders. While in Honolulu I talked to agents in New York and found out the other man in the office with Hanjoi, gave him up and the company brought in a mob hitman to take him out."

"This is all going to wrap up shortly." Doyle said. "Are you two hungry?" he asked Kent and Oscar. They both agreed they were. "Tell your tactical men and the Coast Guard men to come in and eat." An hour later, everyone was full and happy.

"When does your plane take you back from here?" Kent asked Doyle.

"Day after tomorrow, why?"

Kent smiled and said, "I think I'll have my men take the bodies back today, I'll hang around until you, Poppy, and Marge go back and hitch a ride."

"That sounds good to me, too," Oscar said.

187

"Sure and tomorrow we can go find the nude beach," Doyle said with a grin.

"They have a nude beach here?" Oscar said. "I'm not taking off my clothes. No one needs to see me naked."

"And we all thank you for that, Oscar," Marge laughed.

*

Chapter 28

The tactical team took the bodies from the food cooler and brought them to the helicopter. Kent was giving last minute instructions for taking the bodies to the labs for autopsy. He said he'd call and explain what needed to be done with the bodies. Once the FBI men were on the chopper, the Coast Guard men prepared the vehicle for flight. Everyone, including most of the guests on the island were standing by watching the beast lift off and head back to Honolulu.

"Now you're trapped here," Doyle said to Oscar and Kent. "You'll have to watch out for killers."

Doyle made an evil laugh and walked away.

Mr. Dante had his staff put together a pig roast for the guests since they were leaving the next day. Doyle and his party wouldn't leave until the following day, since he paid for one week. This was good, there would be more room on the plane for the extra passengers. Dante said the extra guests were fine with him and offered Albert's sleeping quarters to Kent and Oscar. They agreed.

It was dark now and the former landing area was decorated with TIKI torches, chairs and tables from the hall. A huge pit was open in the ground that was hidden before and a fire set up to roast the pig. The cooking staff cheated a little and prepared the pig before putting it on the spit. Everyone was having a good time.

Marge said, "Now, this is nice," as she watched the pig carcass rotate on the spit.

Lorna was sitting by herself at a table. Marge got up and went to her. "You don't have to be alone now, Lorna. You're a friend, so please join us." Lorna got up and came over to the table where everyone was sitting.

Doyle was watching Marge and smiling. He really was happy that she came to work for him. She was a good person and took care of others. She sat and talked to Lorna.

Kent tapped Doyle on the shoulder and Doyle got up. "What's up?" he asked as they went to the edge of the area, just out of the light.

"Art, did you notice that Dante has been very coy about his staff?" Kent asked.

"Well, he cares for everyone, why?"

"I did some scouting around after our meeting. I thought he was hiding something and he didn't want the police to come to the island. He tolerated me because I was only one man and a friend of yours."

"Okay, so what's your point?" Doyle asked.

"You don't have access to wanted felons and bad guys like I do. I study the mug shots and wanted posters in my spare time."

"You have a sad life, don't you," Doyle laughed.

"Okay, so my social life isn't what you are capable of handling," he said.

"So, get to the point, lonely boy," Doyle said.

"As I said, I did some looking around and found something interesting in the kitchen."

"More dead bodies?"

"No, dummy. A Russian spy," he said and paused.

"What? A spy? I thought we were over that with Russia. They leave us alone and we ignore them."

"Yes, now. But his guy is an old time Russian spy, before the cold war even."

"How do you know?"

"As I said, I pay attention. I also study back through the war books to keep myself busy."

"So, you found a spy, what are you going to do now? Call the State Department and turn him in?""

"He's working for Dante, I wonder if he knows?"

"Well, we could ask Dante."

"You know him better than I do, I'd just frighten him."

"Yes, you have that effect on people. Okay, fine. Let's go find him."

They turned and saw Dante talking to some guests. Probably apologizing for the disturbances during the last week. Doyle and Kent stood nearby and waited for Dante to finish. He smiled and left the people, turning towards the men.

"Mr. Doyle and Agent Simmons. I want to thank you for being discreet about this whole affair," he said with a grin.

"May we talk to you in private?" Doyle asked.

"Certainly. Out here or in my office?"

"How about in the kitchen?" Kent asked.

"Odd request. But sure. Follow me." He went into the building and into the back where the kitchen was. "Now what is so important?" he asked.

Kent pointed to an older man stirring a kettle of some type of food. "Who is that man?" Kent asked.

Dante was surprised by the question and seemed nervous. "He's a long time employee, very good with soups and salads."

"His name, please?" Kent asked.

Dante paused, then let out a big sigh, "You know, don't you?"

"I was suspicious. He's Vladimir Scorpose, correct?"

Dante turned to Kent and said, "He is, but he's not a war criminal anymore. He's been a model citizen for many years. He never killed anyone, just passed information to the Russians about German troop movements. He saved my life, when I was young and in a camp for Polish and Jewish prisoners." He showed them the tattoo on his arm of his number. "He got me out and took me to safety, I owe him my life. If you try and take him away, I'll never forgive you. He's done his penance." Dante looked sad and almost heartbroken.

Kent looked at Doyle. "Well, don't look at me. It's your call," Doyle said in reply.

Kent was doing some heavy thinking. He looked to the old man, weathered by years, working on his foods. "I guess I was mistaken. Sorry to bother you," Kent said and turned away. Doyle followed him out of the kitchen and back to the party.

"I knew you were a softy," Doyle said, following Kent.

"Don't insult me or I'll arrest the man. Now let's drop it."

"Well, now we know why Dante didn't want the police around. He's been secluded on this island for years, hiding the man. I wonder how many other spies he has working here?"

Doyle's Paradise

"Don't even say that. I don't want to know. I want to enjoy my stay in paradise, even for one day. Then I want to go back to civilization, where I can arrest people for spitting on the streets. It's a crazy world out there, Doyle, and you are their leader."

They went back to their friends and sat watching the people enjoying the party. Around eleven it broke up and people wandered off to get some sleep or pack to go back to civilization in the morning.

Marge was drifting off and Lorna gently tapped her. Marge shot up and said, "I didn't do it." She looked around and realized where she was. Everyone laughed and she said she was going to bed. Lorna followed her back to the bungalow.

Poppy was holding Doyle's hand as they sat. "This was a good end to the week. We have one more day here and I intend to find the nude beach. Just to please you," she said.

"I'll have Kent and Oscar come along to give you their opinions."

"You do and I'll never enter your bed again."

Doyle sat quietly. "Well?" Poppy said.

"Okay, I'll keep them away, just you and me, nude on the beach," he said.

"That's better. I don't strip for just anyone."

*

Chapter 29

Kent and Oscar followed David to Albert's sleeping quarters for the night. Doyle led Poppy to their bungalow and decided to go down to the beach. Marge's lights were out so they figured the women were asleep.

They got to the beach and the moon was low and large. A beautiful full moon and it shimmered off the now calm water. Poppy stood next to Doyle and started to undress. Doyle turned to her as she dropped the last of her clothing.

"Why are you taking so long? This was your dream of a nude beach."

Doyle undressed in record time and they stood admiring their bodies. They kissed and caressed each other, then went to the sand and laid down. Doyle was enjoying his dream.

Doyle's Paradise

About an hour later, a storm suddenly whipped up and it started raining, hard. They jumped up, grabbing their clothing and ran to the bungalow. They went in and stood laughing.

"I need a shower. I have to wash out sand where sand shouldn't be," Poppy said and headed to the bathroom.

Doyle was brushing the sand from his body and then went into the shower with Poppy.

They toweled off as the rain still cascaded down the sloped roof. They went to the bed and crawled in, snuggling.

"Well, you got your nude beach wish," Poppy said.

"Yep, with my favorite naked woman," he replied.

They kissed and then finally went to sleep.

The next morning, they were up and getting dressed. Today the plane would fly in to take the guests off the island, and they wanted to watch the exodus.

Doyle planned on keeping Lorna over until the next plane tomorrow. Kent said he'd help her get through the shooting charge.

They went out to find Oscar and Kent talking to Marge and Lorna. "Conspiring so early in the morning?" Doyle asked.

"Just waiting for you two to get your act together and get moving," Kent said. "Dante said the plane arrives by eleven, so we can get some breakfast and go watch."

"I don't think most of these people like me, I was a little rough on them."

"Nobody likes you, Doyle. So you can relax as the departing guests all shoot you the finger," Kent said with a grin. "Then we have to enjoy our last day in paradise. I need to use the sat phone to call my office to arrange for all the stuff we're putting together. Milly left with the chopper back to Honolulu and will type up the testimonies for the record."

"If you have everything pretty well wrapped up, I'd like to get back to Detroit," Doyle said.

Oscar laughed and said, "That's the first time I've heard anyone say they wanted to go to Detroit. Usually they want to get out."

"Yes, but we have a business to run. Our recovery fee won't last forever, we'll need new cases soon. Let's go eat and then go watch people escape from this island."

They had their breakfast and went down to the dock where everyone was gathered with their luggage. They stood back from the crowd and watched as the plane came roaring down from the heavens. It circled once and then came in to a perfect landing on the water.

The staff helped rope the plane down to the dock and proceed to load the bags in the cargo hold. Mr. Dante was up front at the plane's door saying his farewells to everyone as they boarded. Finally the last bag and person were loaded, the door closed and the pilot fired the engines back up. The staff released the ropes and the plane moved away.

The pilot turned it away from the island and throttled up the engines causing the plane to speed up on the water, finally lifting up. It soared away as the last of the guests watched.

Dante and his staff went back to the office, after he waved to them.

"Well, we have the place all to ourselves. Now what?" Oscar asked.

"Take in nature and hike the trails. You may find a body that will require your attention," Doyle said with a grin.

198

"I'll explore, but I better not find a body." Oscar wandered away.

"You know, there's really not much to do in paradise," Doyle said. "They have tennis, shuffleboard and chess, but there are no shops to buy souvenirs, or shows to go to. Not much to do."

"I'm going to take advantage of the beach and swim," Kent said. "I love swimming."

"They have sharks," Doyle said.

"Oh, well, where can one swim?"

David was standing nearby and overheard Kent. "Sir, if you want to swim, I can show you a lagoon that's safe."

"That's what I want to hear, lead on, scout," Kent smiled and followed the boy.

"Do you have swim trunks?" Doyle yelled to him.

"Nope, I swim au naturel," he yelled back.

"Enjoy your swim, we'll go elsewhere. David, keep an eye on him so he doesn't drown."

David waved his reply, and kept going.

Doyle's Paradise

Doyle turned to Poppy, Marge, and Lorna. "Shall we go back to our bungalows and then down to the beach were we can relax?"

They all agreed and went.

The rest of the day was uneventful and quiet. Without the other guests it was deserted. This day gave the staff the opportunity to clean the empty bungalows and change linens.

"Well, tomorrow it will be all over and our vacation will be having to put up with the long flight back home," Doyle said lying on the grass.

"I can fix that," came a voice from behind them. Kent came up looking wet. "I can fly everyone back in the FBI jet as material witnesses. To justify the flight."

"That sounds good, I like it." They turned to see David and Brian carrying a load of firewood and put it down near a fire pit between the two bungalows.

"We'll start a fire for you when it gets dark," David said.

"Where do you get firewood, there can't be that many trees that you would cut down," Poppy asked.

"No, Miss Drake, the firewood is brought in with the ship that brings fuel for the generators and food. We won't cut the palm trees down."

An hour later, they had a roaring fire going and David supplied the women with prongs and marshmallows.

Everyone sat watching the fire and relaxing. Oscar finally joined them from his exploring. Poppy was relaxing on the ground in front of Doyle. She turned to him and said, "This wasn't such a bad trip. The murders were a diversion from the lack of things to do," she paused and looked at Lorna. "Sorry, Lorna, I didn't mean your husband's death was a diversion."

"I understand. I'm not happy about Elmer's death, but it was an exciting adventure," Lorna smiled.

"Yes, quite an adventure," Doyle said watching the fire.

Later, everyone was safely tucked away in their bungalows, packing or sleeping. The next morning arrived and they came out with bags in hand. Lorna said that she didn't want Elmer's clothing, but wanted his personal items. Doyle had them bagged for her.

The security men came and carried their bags to the dock.

David spoke, "I want to say for the men, that it was a pleasure to be under your command. The most excitement we usually get is a drunken guest."

"Glad we could make your week a good one. Good luck running the team, you will do fine."

David grinned and led them to the dock.

*

Chapter 30

They arrived at the dock and got a surprise. The entire island staff, including the old Russian spy, was on hand to bid them farewell.

"Well, this is a sendoff," Doyle said to Poppy. The security men put their bags on the dock and went to stand behind Dante.

"Mr. Doyle and friends," he announced. "I'd like to thank you for everything you've done this week. We all thank you for saving our jobs. This could have been a total disaster if the wrong people had come on the island." Dante nodded to Kent. "We thank you." Before he could finish, the plane roared in and landed. The men went to tie the plane down and put their bags on.

Dante took Doyle aside and reached in his jacket, taking an envelope out. "This is your entire payment for your stay on the island. It's my way of thanking you for keeping control and solving this trouble. And a little thanks for your friend, Agent Simmons, for his discretion about my savior."

"Despite his rough exterior, he has a big heart. Thank you for this. If you ever are in Detroit, look me up."

Doyle reached into a bag he was carrying and took out the satellite phone and charger. "Here, you really need to keep this handy. Find out who the carrier is and start an account. It's my gift for the safety of the people on this island."

"I will. I was wrong to keep totally cut off, as Albert proved. He'd be dead now if it weren't for this phone and you having it. He'll never work again, his brain has complications, but since he has no family, I'll bring him here to live."

Doyle shook the man's hand and they went to the plane. Dante said good bye to each person personally. They boarded the plane and Doyle was looking out the window at the people he had made friends with. David, Brian, the security men, the doctor and all the people he came in contact with. He looked to Poppy and said, "Maybe we'll come here again someday."

"Not right away, please." She let her seat back as the plane leveled out over the ocean.

Kent had arranged for them to ride back to Detroit on the FBI jet from Honolulu and they landed at Metro Airport. Doyle got a cab for him, Poppy, Marge, and Oscar. They arrived back at the office and went in to take a break after the long flight.

"Good to be back," Oscar said. Everyone agreed.

Two days later, Marge was at her desk, Oscar was filling out spousal reports and Doyle was looking out the front window at the traffic.

"Kind of full circle, isn't it?" Marge said from her desk.

Doyle laughed and said, "Yep, I'm back to where it started."

The phone rang and Marge answered. "Hello, Doyle and Drew Investigations, may I help you?" She listened, then said, "Sure, Kent, he's right here. Hold on." She put him on hold and Doyle went to his desk.

He clicked the button to answer. "Kent, how are you?" he said and put the phone on speaker.

"I'm good. We got New York Heavy Equipment and Sales shut down. OCU is exploring their connection to the mob and the IRS has put a hold on all their assets and finances. So Kabe didn't die for nothing."

"What about Lorna?"

"We're not charging her; it was self-defense from my viewpoint. She went back home to start over."

"Good, I feel sorry for her. Maybe I can help her out financially. Get me an address, please."

"I'll email it to you. Janin has confessed with a little help and my persuasion. He was wanted for a number of felonies and he'll be going away for a long while with the murder charges on him. Ballistics on the gun proved it was the murder weapon and Janin's prints were on it. Everything is tied up now so you can relax."

"Thanks, Kent. Are you ready to go back to paradise?"

"Hell, no. I'm staying in Detroit. You can go back to nature," he laughed and hung up.

Doyle's Paradise

The front door opened and Poppy walked in. She said hi to Marge and Oscar then went to Doyle. "How's my nature boy?" she asked.

"Better, now that we're back," he said.

"Anything new about the case?" she asked.

Doyle told her what Kent told him, and they sat in silence for a moment. "I'm glad Lorna is free of charges. She was a sweet girl, really."

"I'm happy that she beat it, too. Now, what are you up to today?" Doyle asked her.

"I was thinking of going to the Detroit Zoo to look at the animals. The ones we didn't see on the island. Care to join me?"

Doyle stood and said, "Maybe they'll have the half-human, half-pig people."

She hit him and went to the door. "Come on pig boy, let's go see your family."

THE END

~~*~~

Bob Moats

Here's a preview of the next book "Doyle's Haunting"

Chapter 1

Marge was thumbing through a scandal magazine at her desk in the office of Doyle and Drew Investigations. She grinned as Oscar Drew came over to drop off some reports he had finished for cases he recently closed. Mostly spousal cheating cases that he enjoyed following. They weren't difficult cases, mostly sneaking around photographing men or women cheating on their spouses.

"Marge, do you really read those trashy things?" Oscar asked her when he saw the paper in her hands.

"Oh, Oscar. I don't believe anything they print, but it's fun to read about all the scandals going on. They're so silly, they can't be real."

"I've skimmed a few of them. My second wife was obsessed by them. She believed whatever they printed. I was glad that she divorced me. I finally burned all the papers she collected."

"I like the stories about the odd creatures around the country. Big Foot in upper Michigan, unicorns in Florida, monkey boys living in a shelter in Maine. It's all so funny."

"Glad you find it funny and not real. It's the people out there that believe that crap that worry me. If they believe that, then they'll believe anything," Oscar said, moving back to his desk.

Doyle's Paradise

"This story is about the ghosts haunting the mansions of Detroit. It's a Halloween special and they say murders have happened frequently." Marge said.

"Marge, there have never been any real reports of ghosts harming humans. The humans hurt themselves running from what they believe were ghosts."

"I know, Oscar. But it's fun to read about them." Marge said.

"Read about what?" Doyle asked coming over from the back of the office, where he was rummaging through the storage space.

"Monsters and ghosts," Marge said.

"Where?" Doyle asked.

"Everywhere. This article is about Detroit. Ghost houses that have been frightening people for years."

"I don't believe in ghosts," Doyle said. "There has never been any real proof that they exist. Lots of people say they have photographed supposed ghosts, but all they had was poor photography and lens flares. If there were real ghosts, they'd take over the world and not just hide in houses, haunting them."

"Ah, a skeptic. If you saw a ghost, would you believe then?" Oscar asked.

"If I saw a ghost, I'd have to investigate it. To substantiate that it's for real and not a hoax or a hallucination."

"When was the last time you hallucinated?"

"I can't discuss that. It was in the sixties and everyone was doing it," Doyle said with a coy smile.

"You were a pot-head? I'm amazed," Oscar laughed.

"I wasn't a pot-head, thank you. Yes, I experimented with certain substances, but only once. Well, maybe twice. There was this girl in Detroit and…"

"Say no more. If a girl was involved, you would have smoked straw," Oscar laughed.

"Let's drop it. Do you have a case to solve?"

"I do and I'm going out now to get on it. Another cheating spouse. You know we're getting quite a reputation for finding evidence of philandering."

"It's the new divorce attorneys I talked to. As much as I dislike them, they keep us busy. They send their clients to us to follow their husbands or wives and we reap the rewards of income."

"Speaking of income, what did you do with the money that Dante gave back to you from your stay in paradise?"

"I sent it to Lorna. She needed to get back on her feet after her husband's murder," Doyle replied.

"That was very nice of you, Arthur," Marge said hearing him.

Doyle's Paradise

"Well, we put the poor woman through hell on the island. It was the least we could do for her. Now can we get back to business?"

Marge giggled and picked up her magazine. Oscar picked up his camera bag and said he was going. Doyle sat at his desk thinking about what he was going to do. The back door opened and Doyle turned, thinking it was Oscar forgetting something. It was Poppy Drake, Doyle's girlfriend.

"Ah, slipping in the back door now?" Doyle smiled.

"I realized that I didn't need to keep coming in through the front door. That's a long walk around the building from the back parking lot."

"I wondered why you kept doing that."

"Hi Margie, how's life after our adventure in paradise?" Poppy said, referring to their trip to the Hawaiian islands, that resulted in a couple murders.

"Nice and quiet," Marge replied. "I even have TV again. You never know how much you miss creature comforts until they're gone. My next vacation will be somewhere there are lots of people having fun."

"I could send you to Las Vegas. There are lots of people having fun."

"I'll consider it. After I save some money," Marge said.

Doyle turned to Poppy as she moved close to him. She leaned down and kissed his lips. "That's a nice way to start the day," Doyle said.

Poppy sat on the chair next to his desk and crossed her beautiful legs. That always distracted Doyle.

"What's up?" he asked, coming out of his thoughts of her legs.

"My company is sending me out to investigate a hotel in Detroit. They claim that a guest was injured by a ghost and they need to cover medical costs."

Doyle looked at Marge when Poppy brought up the ghost subject. Marge was listening, but not showing it. "Your company covers injuries by ghosts? Do all insurance companies have policies for that?"

"No, but it's covered under bodily injuries on premises. They say the reason was the guest claims to have been pushed down stairs by an apparition of an old woman."

"I'd say you have a tough case. The ghost is probably hiding now, so you have to believe the injured woman as to whom the ghost was. Are you going to interrogate the ghost?"

"If I can find it. That's why I came here. I'd like you to come along to help find the ghost."

"Poppy, my dear, I've already discussed this with Marge and Oscar, not more than ten minutes ago. I don't believe in ghosts."

211

Doyle's Paradise

"That's why I want you to go. You are skeptical of most things and you can balance my feelings about spirits."

"Are you saying you believe?"

"I had an experience with a ghost in my youth, yes."

Doyle looked to Marge who was now listening intently. "Did you get that, Marge? We have a real ghost story here. Shall we sit by a campfire and talk of spirits and monsters?"

"Stop making fun. It happened to me and I never forgot it. I was young, but not stupid. And I did see a ghost in my grandparent's house late at night. She came into the room I was staying in overnight and stood staring at me. I couldn't move as she came closer and pointed at me. She moaned and then disappeared. I never knew why she came into the room or why she pointed at me."

"Maybe it was her room and she didn't like you being in it. Ghosts are very territorial from what I hear."

"Maybe so, but I'm not going after a ghost without backup. I figured you were big and strong and could protect me from an old lady ghost."

Doyle sat staring at her, then said, "Marge, hold my calls, I'm going ghost hunting."

Continued in the book.

Bob Moats

The Jim Richards books by Bob Moats

(In series order)

Classmate Murders
Vegas Showgirl Murders
Dominatrix Murders
Mistress Murders
Bridezilla Murders
Magic Murders
Strip Club Murders
Made-for-TV Murders
Mystery Cruise Murders
Talk Show Murders
Sin City Murders
Black Widow Murders
Vegas Vigilante Murders
Area 51 Murders
Mortuary Murders
Hypnotic Murders
Sunshine State Murders
Blue Suede Murders
Honky Tonk Murders
Dark Carnival Murders
Lipstick Murders
Pasta Murders
Talent Show Murders
Shyster Murders
Campground Murders
Network Murders
Reunion Murders
Big Apple Murders
Kennel Murders
Trick or Treat Murders
Santa Murders
Wiseguy Murders
Toxic Murders

For a preview or to purchase a book, go to
http://murdernovels.com

Jim Richards Family of Readers

Thanks to the following people who are now part of the Jim Richards Family of Readers. They have read a book or more and enjoyed them. They all volunteered to be included in the list. If you are a fan of the books, send me your full name and you will be included in future books. Send your name to murdernovels@bobmoats.com to be added here and on the website.

* Achim Feifel * Al Norris * Alex Wheatley * Alexandra Delporte-Wilkinson * Amy Tapia * Andrea Bryan * Anne Shepherd * Arianda Sugar * Arlene Markowski * Ashley Augustus * Audra Hall * Barbara Hughes * Barbara Sammons * Barbara Schuler * Barbara Zirger * Beth Donohue Plenskofski * Beth Rosin * Betsy Childress * Beth Gibson * Bill Sandy * Bill Tornquist * Billie-Jo Collie * Boni J Rychener * Candace Larson * Carl Bishopric * Carla Lewis * Carole Henderson * Carolyn Conroy * Carolyn Riddle-Linington * Cassy Bailey * Cathie Turner * Chad Hudson * Charlie Meier * Charlotte L Duran * Cheryl L. Everett * Cindy Ackley Nunn * Cindy Valstad * Connie Bancroft * Corinne Kay O'Daniel * Dana Robbins Chuchran * Dana Wichita * Daniel Kalus * Danielle Monique * Darren Heald * Dave Travers * David Wilkinson * DeAnn Jannereth * Deanna Miller * Deb Breuker Balbo * Debbie Carter * Debbie White *

Bob Moats

Deborah Fartuch * Deborah Gauze * Deborah Sullivan *
Dee King * Denise Freeman * Diana Carver * Dixie Beck
* Donna Gould * Donna Thompson * Donny Minter *
Doris Kight * Eddie Moore * Eric Walters * Felicia
Annette Bradfield * Francine Menor * Gail Chesney *
Georgiann Minster * George Conner * Greg Colucci *
Hayley Rankin * Harold Garcia * Heidi Arnold * Irma
Ranee Coy * Jacqueline Moss * Jan Kimball * Jane
Lawson * Janice Schneider * Janice Spoor * Jennifer
Redmond * Jerry Dornak * Jessica Keown-Belous * Jim
Beck * Jo Boguslaw * Jo Turner * Joanne Marie Turner *
John Peiffer * John Wisbiski * Joseph Wauro * Joyce
Stacy * Joyce Trifiletti * Judy Franklin * Judy Travers *
Judy Padgett * Julie Heath * Junnahvee Benson * Karen
Dahl * Karen Grams * Karen Higham * Karen Kaiser *
Karen Meinburg Richwine * Karen Kirkman Parker *
Karin Hawkins * Karin Vasvari * Kathleen Donohue
Roesing * Kathleen Riddle-Wolfe * Kathy Hinds Moore *
Kathy Jones * Kathy Mitchell * Katie Benzler * Kay
Burns * Kelly Garcia * Ken Boggs * Keota Rodriguez *
Kiera Mccarthy * Kim Estes * Kimberley May * Kitty
Stolle * Kristie Sciler * Kirsty Stanton * LaLonnie Scallen
* Larry Morris * Leann Parr * Lenora Scales * Leslie
Marie Jackson * Linda Forester * Linda Ingle Cox * Linda
Kennerö * Linda Magill * Lisa Bower * Lisa Keller * Liz
Gibson * Lorraine Wiman * Loretta Alexander * Lynda
Bowles * Lynette Lawrance * LuAnn Louttit * Manny
Rothman * Marcia Gibson DeWitt * Marie Calder *
Marlene Bryan * MaryLouise Kramp * Mary Lynn Gross
* Megan Atkins * Meghan Hyden * Melissa Wescoat *
Melody Cannavan * Michael Carruthers * Michael
Dinkens * Michael Vannoy * Michelle Burns-Mitchell *
Michelle Pilcher * Micki Potter * Mike Moats * Mimi
Baur * Myrna Hecht * Nadine Sutton * Nancy Ellen Sayre
* Natalie Quine * Neena Martin * O'Della Wilson * Pat

215

Doyle's Paradise

Pollington * Pat Rohn * Patricia Jarmon * Patricia C Trezza * Patrick Barry * Paul Lawrance * Peggy Davis * Phyllis Bassett * Raylene Matheny * Rebecca Collins Besner * Renee Brumley * Reta Hanna * Reta Moats * Robert Lenski * Roberta Meister * Roberta Navarro-Harder * Sally Berneathy * Sally Hubler * Sarah Santos * Satka Nikc * Sharon E. Edwards * Sharon Mangini * Sharon McMillon * Sheena Rawl * Sherry Amstutz * Shirley Alvarez * Shirley Davies * Shirley Williams * Stacie Rowe * Stephanie Conner * Steve Cullen * Susan Haughton * Susan Hesse Adams * Susan Salomon * Suzan K Chase * Taisha Cullum * Tamara Moore * Tammy Castleberry * Tammy Lynn Wood * Ted Murphy * Terri Atkins * Terri Creech * Terry Raab * Tonia Rachael Riggs-Williams * Tonya Mann * Travis Fleury-Lopez * Twyla Gawlas * Val Brooks * Walt Munsel * Yvonne Isakson *

Thank you to all these wonderful people.

Thank you for purchasing this book. I hope you enjoy it as much as I enjoyed writing it for my faithful readers. Please feel free to email me to tell me what you thought about my stories. I love hearing from the readers. I can be reached at murdernovels@bobmoats.com thanks again!

*

www.ingramcontent.com/pod-product-compliance
Lightning Source LLC
Chambersburg PA
CBHW070822120626
46556CB00002B/630